# Shaver Mystery Magazine
# Vol 2 No 4 1948

Richard S. Shaver
Alfred Steber (Editor)

SAUCERIAN PUBLISHER
Original Sources in Ufology

**ISBN: 978-1-955087-48-3**

9 781955 087483

2023, Saucerian Publisher

# PROLOGUE

Returning to the classics in any genre is generally a good idea. This also goes for UFO literature. Rereading a book or reviewing old documents after ten or twenty years is a rewarding experience. You will discover new data and ideas you didn't notice before. The reason, of course, is that you are, in many ways, not the same person reading the book the second or third time. Hopefully, you have advanced in knowledge, experience, and intellectual and spiritual discernment. A good starting point is to reread the UFO classics to understand the more profound mystery of what happened during that era.

This title is scarce and hard to find these days. Shaver Mystery Magazine originally was published by the Shaver Mystery Club. This newsletter published the first printed stories on UFOs and was a major forum for debates about the occult, Forteans, and Lemurians. As Ray Palmer promoted it: "dedicated to the further study of the hidden truths as presented in the fact-fiction stories by Richard S. Shaver..."

In essence, the Shaver Mystery is a collection of stories in which Shaver claimed to have discovered proof of an evil humanity in underground caverns. Shaver portrayed an alien race that resided in Earth's caverns before escaping, leaving behind two distinct populations of offspring: the "Teros," a benevolent group of humanoids, and the "Deros," or "detrimental robots," a vile race who tormented and devoured humans. The Deros were especially brutal to women. The tales encouraged the establishment of Shaver Mystery Clubs.

The present edition is an authentic reproduction of the original Shaver Mystery Magazine printed text in shades of gray. **IMPORTANT,even though we have attempted to maintain the integrity of the original work, the present facsimile reproduction may have missing letters and blurred pages, poor pictures due to the age of the original scanned copy.** This magazine has been formatted from its original version for publication. Great, but unpretentious, this issue is an extraordinarily rare symbol of what was going on in those early years of the modern UFO phenomena.

Editor
Saucerian Publisher, 2023

# *The*
# SHAVER MYSTERY
## MAGAZINE

Being dedicated to the further study of the hidden truths as presented in the fact-fiction stories by Richard S. Shaver, made famous in the past three years in AMAZING STORIES magazine.

## Subscription Price 50c per Issue

OBTAINED ONLY

THROUGH MEMBERSHIP

THE SHAVER MYSTERY CLUB

# CONTENTS

VOL. II       1948       NO 4

Frontispiece by Virgil Finlay

## THE SHAVER MYSTERY MAGAZINE

is Published by
THE ALDEBARAN PRESS
BOX 158, McHENRY, ILLINOIS

# ❧ EDITORIAL ☙

This is the first issue of the magazine wholly prepared by myself. It will get better. If I recover.

I want more copy from members. The Club can't pay for such copy yet, but it looks as if we were going to be able to do so. And you who find that fifty cents a burden can wangle a subscription at least for some good copy. Rev. Irene Farrier has earned quite a number of subscriptions (she didn't expect payment of any kind) with her voluntary library research in quest of items interesting to the Club. If a Reverend can find time to help, so can you. One or more of them will appear next issue. Whether you want subscriptions or not, please put some time on such work.

Members in New York held a meeting which some forty-two attended, if I recall correctly. I will give any members who desire to organize such meetings all the help I can. I get constant requests for the names of neighbour members, and you members who cherish isolation will have to remind me not to give out your names to those who want to look up other club members in their neighbourhood.

This issue contains some pretty potent corroboration for all the basic truths-in-question of the Shaver-Mystery. If only the correspondents would allow me to give their names and addresses, such corroboration would bear more weight. When you can do so, please omit that postscript that cuts off permission to use your name. In the case of the psychic school teacher, however, we forgive you. It's weighty, anyway.

Next issue is really going to be a humdinger. I think you will say it is the best issue so far. Also it very nearly winds up "Mandark", and I want you readers to fill the gap with some first class material.

Aldebaran Press and Shaver Mystery Magazine are pretty well married now, to answer several queries if they were the same. Reason for the different names and the P.O. Box is that I want at some future date to turn the magazine over to some organized group of the club to put out as a bona-fide club organ, rather than a one-man ambuscade of the learned dim-wits who have got us all into our condition of supreme ignorance.

In Aldebaran Press I have commercial partners. In Shaver Mystery Magazine I have only you members as partners and I hope the magazine will become yours when you are ready to handle it. Is that clear? Then don't write me a raft of letters demanding an answer about it, I am only one man.

I have now gotten hold of some copies of Science Comics and lost the letters asking about them. I only file letters about business and make notations about subscriptions on file cards, so I guess a lot of you will have to repeat that request.

I want you members to set up Club Hdqtrs. to handle the correspondence and filing of all items of research, investigation and technical angles of this thing. The New York, Phila. and Detroit members are getting this done, but California, where the greatest number of you live, lags behind. Chicago has a felon on his finger and a certain book I need, and I impatiently await his visit as my wife approves and will cook a good dinner. Nearly sixty members in Chicago and no meetings! It would be a wonderful excuse to get out for the evening, too. Bill, get busy.

Flying saucers are still alien space ships.

                                                            Richard S. Shaver

# READER'S SECTION

**Each issue we will publish as many pertinent letters to the Shaver Mystery as space allows. We urge all readers to contribute any facts, personal or otherwise, to help our research.**

Malden, Mass.
May 23, 1948

Dear Mr. Shaver:

Now that I have finished volume 4, I should like to make a few comments on it. This letter may be long so I advise you to lay it aside until you have time to take in its contents (A friendly warning!).

First, do you realize that there are people receiving the little magazine who are totally incapable of being useful to us since they are fully controlled by "tamper" at the present time? One such has tried to sell me on the idea that the whole thing is a hoax and that you are (To express the thought in my own words) "The World's biggest and worst liar!" Needless to say, this does not deter me in my faith in what you say as I am a living proof of the fact that there ARE "tero" at the controls of *some* of the "mech" in the caves!

Yes! Other than the evil thoughts I have had implanted in my mind (And of which I wrote you some time ago), there are other—er, what (?), that are beneficial to me that have reached me and done what modern science has been unable to do—though even the cave cure, if such it is, is not permanent at present, but must be aided by surface science at the present time. I shall soon be well. This was promised only last night during a treatment from the caves. This is no hoax, I know what has been done, I asked for it and got the treatment I needed!

Now to get at the real purpose of this letter. Mr. Howard MacDonald of New York seems to feel that you cannot be taken seriously if you have spent time in jail! Mr. MacDonald, let me caution you, DON'T read the Bible, some of its books were written by "jail-birds" too! And good Heavens! Don't go near a copy of "Pilgrim's Progress" it was WRITTEN IN JAIL! So what? The idea is O.K. isn't it?

When do we start on Copeland's idea?

Cuthbert—you better read MANDARK *now*—surprising how it applies to TODAY!

You, Mr. Shaver, are right about the ray in this section. Mostly we have "de" ray in this section, but just recently there has been a very evident influx of "tero" ray that seem to be counteracting some of the tamper and we are able to think more clearly hereabouts, thank the powers that be, and I note the change in ALL people, not just a few—surface man is still essentially GOOD if given a chance to be away from the tamper of rays. It is so in this area, at least.

Speaking of Jap beliefs on the caves—there is an amazing agreement in Germany also. German's "in the know" believe in a cave group and Ethereal beings and even assign a "landt" to them—somewhere in space. They have a belief in a being even superior to Yahveh, whom they call Otl (Look that up in Mantong—and gasp, as I did when I got home!), who is the father of Yahveh and evidently a "bio-chemist" by the common standard of today!

It is surprising, to me, that you should be taken as all sorts of a liar and other things not pleasant. Those that doubt you, however, appear to be those unable to grasp the fundamental point of the story, who see only the fiction in the stories and not the real points you try to bring out (Could this be more "tamper"?). People ask for proof of your claims. What is needed? Must a ton of bricks land on a person's head to make them realize that there are bricks in the world? Many will admit that there is something to the idea of dinosaurs, yet try to say that this is perfectly consistant with all the Bible says. True. Then how does Shaver discredit that Book? Because he has added a few more years to the age of man? Is that bad? Would man rather be a monkey instead? Winston Churchill, the author, once called man, "Homo Stultus", science says, "Homo Sapiens", let man prove who is right by his ability to THINK and arrive at a LOGICAL conclusion without allowing the issue to be beclouded with such questions as, "Is Shaver a Jail-bird?" Bah! Churchill has two strikes on science now! Even science has conceded three points of the four point claim of Shaver, but common man says, "feed me some more monkey glands!"

Some thinkers, however, are not so blind, Mr. Shaver, (Witness the "roundtable" in the last issue.) so there is SOME SLIGHT hope, but will we be too late? If there is a spark of the ancient "godhood" of old left in man, let us pray to the Supreme Being that that spark may be rekindled into a flaming torch of desire to seek and find the truth, no matter where the search

Continued on Page 36

# MANDARK

## By RICHARD S. SHAVER

### Continuing the tremendous 200,000 word Novel
### - - - the true story of the Life of Christ

*The third portion of this book will be devoted to a fictionalized picture of the cavern life of today.—In the first was a short fictionalized picture of the cavern world as it was when it was abandoned by the Elder race, followed by a picture of the strange, probable origin of the human race according to the traces of that time still obtainable in the thought-records—followed by a picture of the caverns under Jerusalem at Christ's time, plus various extensive explanations of the caverns as they have been used and lived in traced from extant readings and writings of various men of the surface.*

*Since the second part was a picture of the caverns at Christ's time—it is fitting the book conclude with a picture of the cavern life today, what it is—what it intends to be with surface man—how they live, look and act—why they are still a grave threat to all progress. Why they still monopolize the whole vast miracle of the machinery of the caverns that could be of such terrific inestimable value to surface science were it understood and acquired for exploration and study—or even one small bit of that machinery acquired—is the thing that is explained in this later third of the book. Why this explanation is important, and why it must be understood and believed so that men will search and try until they do obtain some of the antique mechanisms for the sake of the race of man. That is why this latter part is important—and please do overlook the effects of strain and weariness and other ill-influences which has made this book so much less than it was desired to be. For it was written through and against constant tamper and obstruction from the mad wights of the caverns, and with the help of the sane grey people of that strange, fierce world of utter darkness or weird lights from the dynamos of the Gods.*

## CHAPTER VIII

### —End of Yahveh's Records—

(Continuing the account of Nydia and her records)

I CAME out of the trance of the records, that trance called "dream" by the underworld, but which is vastly more than dream—to see the face of my Nydia smiling down upon me. She released from my head and arms the wires and attachments of the "dream-mech" and I got up and stretched. It seemed to me that life-times had elapsed since I sat down—but in reality I suppose not more than four or five hours had passed.

"Now you understand some little of the history of the caverns. The whole story is so vast, and the area of the caverns is so vast, the conditions of life so variant in the different areas which are inhabited, the people so very different from each other and from surface man—that the whole story is really too great for any modern man to grasp. But we can get a glimpse of it, and such a glimpse I have given you."

"What happened to that area under Jerusalem after Yahveh left Earth?"

"I will show you a modern record of a certain event under Jerusalem. It is only a few months old, and was sent us by our friends in Europe. We circulate these records as you surface people do books, you know—it is one of our few ways of keeping track of what goes on in the underworld. That and continual chatter over the relay lines— by which we are able to talk around the world by means of our telaugs from one to another—and like a grapevine it is surprisingly efficient at times, and at other times the most important news fails to come through at all."

Centuries have passed over Jerusalem the Golden, time, the crusades, wars upon wars—Jerusalem lies—an old woman in the sun—a dirty old woman begging—and the year is 1946.

Derek Verne—ex-marine—had decided to take up the profession of treasure hunting. It is a profession that attracts certain men. Men who know all the lore of out of the way places, who have looked upon old maps that have led other men to treasure—men who have talked to that little known guild of highly specialized training—requirements.

F. MAGARIAN

Derek Verne had inherited the nose for treasure from his father. This natural bent had been given a great impetus by a buddy in the army. He had died in Italy—but he had left to Verne a memento—a very old map. The map had been a picture of a Jerusalem—and on the outskirts, a certain Wadi—called "Wadi El Yahveh"—was marked in red ink. With the map, was a letter written to Verne by his buddy from the hospital where he had lain dying of a belly wound that would not heal. The letter said—

*"Dear Pal:*

*I know you have a yen for treasure hunting and the times you and I shot the bull over the tall yarns of those hard bitten guys who spend their lives chasing the red gold through the forgotten places of the world were some of the best times of my life, believe it or not. So few guys know the real lore of that kind of life, know the tales of the treasure hunters—and I am kinda sorry I never showed you this map or told you the story myself. It gives the location of a steep old shaft outside of Jerusalem. The story behind this shaft is unbelievable—but so are most of the stories guys like you and I follow to their source—to find the source genuine and the story a true one. The old tale tells that the shaft leads to the abode of "devils"—but very rich devils—who live in golden rooms deep under the surface of Jerusalem. These devils are supposed to be the descendants of a bunch of ancient racketeers who used to pretend to be gods and get all the golden gifts the temples took in from the gullible. The kind of guys who performed miracles for the temples so the flow of coins would come in faster.*

*The tale has a lot more to it than that but I don't have the time or strength to write it all out—I am sure going to be dead before very long—they ain't fooling me.—I can tell when the nurse walks softer every day, as well as the next one! I know! In case I don't die, I will want this back—but there aint much chance of that. As a last request— I ask you to go down in that strange shaft and get to the bottom and see just what is there. If I can I'll come back and haunt you just to find out what is down there—and you better be ready to tell my ghost all about it, buddy. You're the best pal a guy ever had, and if I know anything about treasure maps, this is the best gift a dying man could give his best friend.*

*Good luck, you old son of a cross-eyed quarter-back.*

*So long, buddy—*
*Jack Requan."*

## THIRD PART
### CHAPTER 1

VERNE tried, but it was no go. Every muscle bulged and he had plenty of them to bulge. But the terrible thing would not move. He had to move it or die—and it would not move. It would not . . .

He would have given that straining right arm for a crowbar. But as he looked desperately around, nothing presented itself. That black, hot nothing, dry and dusty, that pervades the deeper caverns of earth. That *nothing* that can be so intrusive, so sentiment, yet is in truth black nothing!

There was left him no course but to wander off into that blackness on and on . . . Into those interminable burrows . . .

He had glimpsed the dust-shrouded shapes of weird machinery as the falling rock had blocked his place of entrance, crushed out his head-lantern. He knew he was at last inside the buildings, the endless, forgotten, titanic burrowings of those legendary gigantic men of the past, the Elder Gods who had left earth so long ago. He had hardly believed in them before, though he had agreed to lead the expedition to attempt an entrance to the God-caverns because he had read enough to know that such wonders *must* exist somewhere on earth. There were so many references to them in old writings! So many miracles explainable in no other way than by the marvelous machines of some superior race, who, since they did not exist in the present, must have lived on earth in the past. Too, he had Requan's letter!

So he had agreed to accompany the expedition to enter that smooth, utterly mysterious shaft in the Wadi El Jahveh which no one had ever followed to the bottom. It went in on a slant, down and down, and no rope, no dropped rock, had ever sent back an echo that said—"this is the bottom." So he, Derek Verne, had agreed to help with the expenses and to lend his strength to an attempt to see if these *were* the lost caverns written of by Shaver and many another writer of the past—the caverns of the Fey, of the Gods of the Underworld, of the Styx, of the Hell of the Norse—of all those tales from the past which tell us of the strange realm under the earth.

Six of them, roped together, had slid down that endless shaft, dragging after them one mile of wire—and if it were deeper than a mile—there were other great spools adjacent, to attach to the end. Over this wire they could talk to the surface. Down and down the shaft had led—and at last the opening into the side for which they had hoped had appeared.—They would not have to plumb that strange shaft clear to the mysterious bottom, for an opening had appeared into which they had crawled to gain time to cool their friction heated feet, their burned hands and change their scorched gloves. Getting out, they knew, was going to be some problem, after that slide down. But they knew all civilization could be summoned by their friends on the surface if they failed to make good on that climb back up the chute of smooth, strange rock.

They had entered that ragged hole in the side of the shaft, six of them, to see if it were by chance what they were hoping for, an entrance to the legendary underworld, which they hardly believed in—but which so many indications in their researches had led logic to insist must exist. Six of them, and now only he was left—Derek Verne the strongest and youngest of those six. Chance had dropped that rock upon them just as their lights had revealed where the rough passage led into a strange, weird, vast chamber, filled with dust shrouded shapes suggesting age-old machinery. Derek, in the lead, had pushed through the narrow opening into the strange chamber—and then with a rumble, the roof had dropped upon his companions, leaving him alone in the dark with the terrible cries of his companions suddenly cut off—still ringing in his brain. The dark, and those sudden, quick cries echoing in his memory.—The dark and his two hands, his strong young body, were all he possessed, now. The wire to the surface lay somewhere beyond that rock fall, and pressing down on those rocks that had dropped was God alone knew how much weight from above.

His equipment, and that of his friends, lay at the other end of that short passage where they had left it, for they meant to take a quick look into this passage, and then continue with the descent of the smooth, strangely artificial shaft which had led them to their death, thought Derek, sadly.

Well, if there was anything to find in that wilderness of strange shapes—anything of value to that twentieth century civilization upon the sunny surface, anything there that careless disregard of the past was overlooking—he would find it. But how could he tell them, would he ever get out of this darkness again? Logic told him with its inexorable voice that he was as good as dead now. But life surged within his veins, told him with better logic that while there was life there was hope.

He had better find what there was to find soon. The first requisite was water. Second requisite—light. Third was food.

If that great chamber of dust-shrouded shapes he had glimpsed just as the falling rocks had dashed his lamp from his head and given him that goose-egg that throbbed on his forehead—if that chamber was a cavern home of that legendary race of the Gods —then they must have had water in their dwellings. If they had water down here, there must be pipes, fountains, something. He would look, with his bare hands in this pressing darkness—for water.

He turned from the immovable rock that had crushed down upon his chances of regaining the surface world—and step by step—his hands outstretched before him to ward off a bump against those crouching metal shapes—he advanced into the dry, hot darkness—into that grey blanket of age-old dust his feet pushed, step by low step. The dust rose, choked his breathing, he coughed—but kept on.

Logic told him the water-pipe would be at the wall of the chamber. Safety for his shins and his life told him the wall was the safest way to progress. So, now his hands felt carefully over the surface of the wall—up,—down—and on into the dark.

Under that soft, choking dust that his every movement seemed to cause to dissolve into the air under his hands—he noticed at last a roundness—a coldness in this hot dryness. He felt around the projecting thing upon the wall. Its shape told him little, except that it seemed the sculptured head of an animal. Still his hands explored the thing, and under that projecting visualized mouth of the sculptured animal, his hands found a great bowl, inset in the wall—a bowl that his imagination leaped to tell him might have been the receptacle of a wall fountain. But wall fountains were things that flowed steadily, and from the mouth of this animal flowed no water—his hands felt of the cool mouth of metal, felt of the teeth projecting sharply—and drew back as if stung as they felt a cold slimy wetness!—He screamed, his nerves at the breaking point, it felt like the cold skin of a snake! He stood there for long moments, quieting his nerves, then with an effort his hand explored the strange opening in the metal projection again, and again he felt the dampness that should not be there—was alien to that dry heat.

He drew in his breath with a sharp gasp. That dampness was water drops, and now his ears detected what his hands told him must be there, a slow drip, drip of water. Swiftly his hands flew in the dark to the bottom of that metal basin under the metal head, and there in the hole the centuries of dropping water had worn in that hard metal, was a little pool of water, a line of dampness where to it trickled back—back—to a hole very like a drain-pipe opening. Whatever this thing was in the light, in the dark it gave him all the sense impression of a wash bowl and a leaky faucet.

His first need was filled. He had here a supply of water, for the steady drip told him there was quite enough for him, and his hands told him the little basin the dripping had worn in the metal would always hold a cup of water ready for him. Now, his logic told him to avoid losing that precious supply, and Derek sat down in the dark, and after thinking a moment, took off a sock, began swiftly to unravel it. He tied one end of the thread to the metal, rolled the rest into a ball. He had decided to limit his explorations for the present to the limit of that ball of cord from one sock. He had heard too many stories of death by thirst to want to experience such a death.

Now, light? His mind leaped to the thought "Since my former deductions as to the nature of this place proved correct, and the wall did hold a water source—perhaps further deductions of the same nature might prove correct. Since the wall seemed to hold an aperture for water, perhaps it also holds something in the form of light—a switch.—Derek laughed. A light switch down here where no man had been for untold centuries, for perhaps thousands of years—tens of thousands—It was too ridiculous, but his hands, obeying the leaping hope in his heart roused by the finding of water, kept on persistently exploring the wall. They must have had light, perhaps torches stuck in the wall—something might turn up—on the wall!

Not far from the basin of metal in which the water dripped, dripped, somehow telling with each slow drop of the awful time that had passed—not far from that drip, under that grey blanket that clung there even to the vertical, unnaturally smooth wall— his hands struck an excrescence—an alternately smooth and rough surface, a large patch of strangely irregular projections. Swiftly his fingers, made wise by the necessity in the darkness, felt about the thing, and in the center of the shield-shaped strangeness was a little projection the size of a thumb. His hands tugged hopefully at it, just as they had tugged at the light switch at home when the darkness made his rooms strange to him.

And just as it had at home, at the tug and click came light. Not the same kind of light, but a weird glow swiftly flooded through the vast chamber, and his eyes, blinded— closed in spite of him against the wonder that leaped at them.

But not for long. He tugged his eyes open in spite of the sensation after the long dark—and looked about him wildly, hopefully, saying—with swift wonder and glad, overwhelming surprise—"It's all true—true . . . The home of the Gods—the Elder world—its true—I have found it."

A strange, weird echo of his voice rebounded, seeming to say in tones not his own —"He has found it, poor boy. He has found it! May the Gods help him." But somehow this wonder of an alien, pitying voice was overwhelmed and hidden for him by the wonder of what his eyes were telling him.

The metal projection from which the water dripped was the sculptured head of an animal—a strange weirdly beautiful head too, and the water from it dripped into the metal basin of a fountain. The light was of several separate colors, distributed about the chamber in a theatrically designed way, so as to light up certain things, and this gave Derek a thought. He touched the button again, and mysteriously—immediately, the whole vast chamber took on a new, different, even more startling appearance. To get his eyes under that blanket of grey dust and see what was there, that was able to suggest so much in that light without one being able to actually see the details—

Derek took his gloves, set busily to work brushing off the nearest forms under the green, hidden light that was behind it.

Sculptured metal came slowly to meaningful form under his ministrations—and when he was through, two great statues of metal loomed at each side of a vast enigmatically beautiful machine. What it was, what it was designed to do, how to operate the thing—Verne had no idea—but that it was the work of beings more than human he had not the slightest doubt.

He stood examining the fearful wonder of the great, too beautiful machine, with its sparkling, engraved surface, so beautifully telling of loving careful work by hand craftsmen greatly more than human in their dexterity and art sense. As he stood rapt in a curious exaltation before the work of what he knew now was the ancestors of all men . . . a fear struck into him at a movement—a grey, careful movement just beyond his line of vision. His eyes darted into the shadows, and a cry rose to his lips, only to be shut off by his hand.

For within the shadow cast by the great machine stood a little naked grey man, with huge eyes staring at him. He seemed as startled at first as Derek himself—but he cast off his fear with a shrug—did the little grey man, and stepped forward, holding out his hand palm upward in a gesture familiar yet alien—as though he meant to shake hands with this stranger because he knew Verne expected it—yet never having shaken any one's hand, just didn't know exactly how to go about it. Verne found his voice and said—

"Now, who in H—— are you . . . ?"

The little man stood for an instant in thought, as though wondering how to tell Derek, then his mouth opened, and what seemed a little used and rusty voice said— "I am one who lives . . . here."

"Alone—you live here all alone?"

"No, not alone. Many people live near. I come for you—sent to bring. I speak your language easily, they sent me. You will learn. Don't ask questions, come and learn."

Derek Verne followed the grey figure as it retreated into the shadows and an eery creeping sensation swept over his body, the sensation that sometimes strikes a man when he sees an amputation or a cripple—pity and something else, something alien and mutilated about the man. But he followed him. His thin legs moved briskly off, raising little clouds of dust with each step. As they moved down the vast corridor that Derek now found opened off the great chamber, the dust grew gradually less, till after fifteen minutes walking, the dust had disappeared from under-foot, and the great gleaming walls stood revealed in all their vast beauty. Derek gasped as they passed wall lights which fully revealed the otherwhere shadowed paintings and bas-relief sculptures on the walls. For they were pictured life—a life as far beyond a man's imagination as truth itself.

The little grey man drew aside presently into an opening, and Verne followed. He stopped then, with a kind of disappointment at the opposite sort of greeting from what he expected, here in this wonderland of the past great of earth—For, squatted around the wall in a gloomy silence, were a score of people, various—silent, half-naked or naked —, grey, or white with a fish-belly whiteness,—hardly curious as he stepped in with his normal surface clothing and bronzed skin setting him so apart from them. One grey, sharp-faced girl, squatting nude by the fire that glowed in the center of the great, beautiful room, stirred rather sulkily an iron pot from which an odor of stew drifted with the fire smoke. She glanced at Derek, estimated his value as a man, winked at him slightly— covertly, went on stirring. Derek stood—non-plused. No fuss—accepting him as an every day occurrence in their lives—it was too much for him!

"What is this? Do you people have visitors every day—or are you just naturally impolite—or are you tired? I don't get this. I come into a place I think uninhabited, the prime wonder of the world, and instead of emptiness and the starvation I expect I find people—people so used to men like me they hardly glance at me. I couldn't be differently received if this was Broadway, New York. Could someone give with the information?"

The girl at the pot, as no one spoke—glanced again at him and said matter-of-factly—"This stew is ready, come and get it. As for you, stranger, sit down and make yourself at home. You'll be a long time here. You might as well get used to it. Just because you stumbled in here by accident, don't think you are "out of this world." You don't mean any more to us than any other poor goof from the surface. Sit down, I'll bring you a bowl of stew. And take care of your bowl, you may need it again."

Derek sat down. It was too much for him.

The stew was good. Derek washed his bowl in the wall fountain as he saw the others do, then stacked it in a great wall cupboard like the others. He went and sat down again. Presently the girl went to another wall cupboard, slipped on a torn dress, not too clean—and came and squatted by him against the wall. Derek waited, he wasn't biting on this silent treatment again. Enough was enough.

"You're the guy from the "expedition." The rest were killed by a rock fall just as they found "crawly-way?" Is that right?"

"That's right, how did you know?"

"Oh, we heard about your expedition before it ever left the surface, in fact, before you even left your home last week. Don't you really know who we are?"

"No, but I'll bite. Who are you?"

"I guess you'd call us the "nameless people." But we know all about the surface people. Watch?" The girl got up, went to one of the great machines that here shone in a polished, dustless splendor, and flipped a switch. A screen glowed with deep color, and on the screen appeared a scene in the forest above, the green leaves glistened with a recent rain, the sun shone brightly, and from the screen a bird sang its sweet refrain on the beauty of the day.

"See. That's how we know what goes on up above. We know a great deal more about your life than you do; hence our boredom—our lack of interest in you and your "startling" appearance among us. We have other people from the surface with us. Over there sits one now."

Derek's eyes followed her pointing finger, and there in the corner crouched a man in clothing like his own, but far gone in disrepair—several years ago those clothes might have looked serviceable—but now they hung in rags, and his toes peeked from the ends of his shoes. Trousers, shirt, tangled hair uncut, he looked his weariness with life at Derek, did not speak. A hopeless set of faces these people had, they looked at Derek, but appeared too weary to care whether they thought about him or not.

"Just what ails them all?" Derek asked the girl. "This isn't natural. I never saw people less interested in living."

"Did you ever see slaves before?" The girl asked the question of Derek with a knowing glance into his eyes, a glance that told him a lot more than she perhaps meant to tell him.

"They're not slaves? Slaves . . ." Derek saw a great light. The weariness, the boredom, the hopeless expressions. The lack of clothes—though in this dry heat no clothes were vastly more comfortable than any—Derek realized, wiping the sweat from his eyes.

"Yes, we are slaves and so are you—though you don't know it yet. You can only hope to be a slave here, chances are you will get the arena—Did you ever hear of an arena?"

"An arena? You mean, like the Olympic arena—a place for games—football, etc? What do you mean, "I'll get the arena?""

"I mean the Roman type of arena—where people fight with wild animals or each other—where women fight with bare hands against pythons—such-like entertainments— ever see a Roman arena?"

"I begin to know what you mean. You mean this place is ruled by a cruel tyrant— a person who has made slaves of you all—who makes people fight to the death in an arena for his amusement."

"That's the general idea."

"Well, why don't you help me remove that stone from the place where I entered? We can go back out—walk right up to the surface and away. No slavery on the surface. Hah!"

"It aint that simple, friend. I aint got time to explain it all to you, my shift starts in ten minutes, I gotta go. Just wait right here, and soon they'll send for you. I just got time for a little advice which I know you won't follow. No matter what they say— don't get mad! Don't even let your voice show anger. And don't try to do anything— fight back or sock somebody or anything. They'll give you the arena. But if you're smart—tell them you know something about juice—you know, an electrical engineer. They give those guys a better berth than us poor dumb slaves. See! So long now— hope I see you again."

Derek felt a wrench of fear, the only person who had shown the slightest interest in him was now walking out of the cavern, her young and not unlovely figure hardly hidden by the torn garment she had put on. Derek called after her.

"Girl—girl—what is your name?" She looked back and grinned almost shyly.

"The name is Mary—Mary Jakeman. I'll be seeing you. Don't worry, it won't help you any." Her somehow capable and trim figure disappeared briskly through the doorway. How could a girl in a torn dress and nothing else, an old grey, dénim dress, too—how could she manage to look capable and brisk. Derek guessed it was by comparison with these other gloomy customers sitting big-eyed and listless about the room. Their thin grey limbs and child-like bodies, sparse hair, an alien under-nourished, almost dwarfish appearance marked them to Derek as the real natives of this underworld life. He attempted to strike up a conversation with the thin, sad looking individual next to him. He was wearing only a pair of thin, tan linen pants, his feet were bare. Verne asked —"Been here all your life?"

"Aw, skip it. I know every question you're gonna ask me before you open your mouth. Why bother, you'll learn if you live so long. There's nothing to tell you that'll make you feel any better."

"Since you keep telling me there's no hope, and you all look so hopeless—could you loosen up enough to tell me why you're all so gloomy and quiet? I just don't get it."

"Look, bud, we used to amount to something, years ago. We lived a wonderful life, how wonderful you can't understand until you know more about this life. And don't get the idea because we're small and thin and different that we're inferior. Most of us have always despised the surface people, it's an old custom to make fun of your race. Lately we wish we hadn't made quite so much fun—and made more use of your wits—which I'll admit are of a different type from our own. Now—we're slaves, and plenty of you guys come down here and become slaves too. Especially your women."

"Go on! You started talking, keep on. It's better than sitting there staring at this wonder work as if it were your coffin. How come you talk so much like people do on the surface—as you call it?"

"We talk that way because we always have watched you and talked to some of you, listened to all of you—all our lives. We feel bad right now because we all got a bad break not long ago, and it aint setting none too well. We hate to talk to you because we can't help thinking of the fun we used to have when we got a new-chum down here and initiated him—and we hate to tell you what's really in store for you."

"What is in store for me?"

"The thing that aint really human, the thing that made slaves out of some of us, and dead ones out of the best of us—is going to call you in for an interview. And if I say any more to you—I'm liable to get the same medicine you'll probably get. Can you get it? We don't like to talk—it gets us in bad—cause when a guy talks, he says what he thinks, and when he keeps quiet, he can keep from thinking what he hates to think of anyway. See!"

"I get a faint glimmer. O.K.—Have it your way. I'll learn the hard way."

"It'll be hard, brother, but that's the way it is. We're mostly human, but some things on earth aint exactly what I'd call human. Not so's you could notice it. And one of them things took over here not long ago. Too long ago . . . Too darn long ago . . ."

Derek lapsed into silence and his companion fell into a doze, sliding down from his crouch against the wall, his head lolled sideways, he snored. He seemed to be exhausted. Derek sat and looked at the others—some dozen of them now. Women, frail, thin-armed, grey-skinned, ribbed and lean as though hungry for too long—they squatted and hugged their knees, or lay on thin pallets on the floor and slept open-mouthed. There was no talk—now and then one came in—nodded to another—one went out. Suddenly he jumped as a sharp needle, red hot, seemed to sink into his arm. He jumped to his feet, glared around. No one was near. A voice from that no-one sounded in his ear. "Come along, you!"

"Come along where? I'm new here! I can't see—anyone!" A little shiver ran through Derek Verne, it was uncanny, somehow—that voice. It was all a little too darn hard to understand.

The voice said "Move!—I'll tell you where to turn. Like this!" . . . and Derek leaped a foot in the air as a sharp pain seared into his buttock. "Now move, you fool! You'll catch on."

Derek moved, toward the door and started to turn right in the great corridor. But again the pain seared his shoulder, he turned left and started walking. The pain struck into his buttock again—"Faster! I haven't got all day." Derek walked faster. He was learning. You couldn't argue with this thing. You had to obey. He was beginning to understand the hopeless apathy, the resignation in the faces of those people in their great chamber—those people so alien, yet somehow vaguely familiar, as though he had known them all in dreams somewhere. He had. They had made many dreams for him all his life and knew him well. But Derek didn't know that, yet. He only sensed it.

The burning ray drove him along like a whip in an expert hand, down corridors and turns in the vast warren of beauty indescribable that this place was to him whose eyes had never seen the home of the Gods. As he passed along the endless sculptures and vaulting domed roofs covered with paintings no man could ever hope to even understand, he could not help but see the terrible marks of vandals—effaced and illegible antique writings on the walls, places where apparently explosives had been used to burst open some store room doors, a ruin it was from such work—but a still habitable and infinitely beautiful ruin. Now the corridor widened, the roof went up and was lost in the gloom, and in a great bowl before him loomed a vast building that seemed more like a great machine—a vast square loom of metal, ringed about with strange coiling of six inch thick cables, of six foot pipe that entered its sides—and over the whole vast machine-like building quivered and danced an electric aura of powerful beauty—that seemed to be the distilled electric essences of beauty, mingled and made to dwell there by some magic holding of the electric fields from those vast coiling cables throbbing with power flows. The place drew Derek as a moth is drawn by flame, as a child is drawn by a mother—nay, it drew him more as a soul is drawn by its God, irresistibly—electrically, overwhelmingly—his self-control went from him, and he ran up the great two foot high steps and into the great arching metal doors that swung open to admit him . . . Ran, with a kind of puppy whimpering, into that terrible yet beautiful generator of the essence of life-force, and the beauty of life force—ran into what seemed as he entered, the arms of God himself.

The vital electric aura thickened about him as he entered the doors and an overwhelming thrilling of pleasure throbbed steadily through his limbs, so that they quivered steadily, as a dog's hind end quivers from the wagging of its tail. But sometimes the dog is kicked . . .

Through that throbbing, irresistible vibration of powerful pleasure impulses Derek Verne walked, to meet the ruler of this place so far beneath earth's surface. His mind no longer wholly his own, for the man new to synthetic pleasure vibrants in great quantities cannot truly think when subject to such flows—Derek stood at last, within that place that had evidently once been the center dwelling of this vast home of the Elder race —that had been the Nirvana in which some mighty being of the far past had lived in such pleasure for years called by us immortal in number.

Derek stood now before a number of people, and his mind numbed and swooning from the pleasure vibrants that bathed this whole place of golden metal, of yellow metal of some kind—that throbbed through the air constantly—his mind tried to see and grasp what was here—what was this thing upon the throne—this ruler whom the slaves outside had warned him not to anger—

She was seated on a vast coruscating metal seat, surrounded—the seat was—by a sculptured leaping and weaving of lovely antique figures, giants and giantesses interwoven in a play of immortal form.—It was beauty, immortal's handiwork, that throne, but Derek's eyes were drawn from it to the figure that sat in the ruby stone of the seat, frowning down upon him where he stood, himself dwarfed to insignificance by the terrible, awesome splendor of the place. This figure was an old, a terribly old woman. Her hair, white as snow, was dressed high, as in the days of Louis 14th, and the towering head of hair was hung with startling colors, gems glittering in ropes upon it. Her arms and shoulders were bare, old and wrinkled—but yet soft and white with care, and Derek wondered how many slaves had massaged and oiled those arms how long, how many years—how old *was* she? She did not smile, her face frowned absently at him, and Derek could not help wondering why she looked so vacant-eyed—so somehow violated, as though her mind were not "absent", but somehow "removed." Her dress, a glittering silver cloth of some metallic sheen, as though hung with tiny sequins, embraced her still slender and nearly youthful figure gracefully. Her hands, small and very quick— caressed a great feather fan. About her leaned a group of people, and as Derek's eyes ran over their faces, he rememberd the slave beside him in the place where he had waited before being brought here—"Some things—some people, just ain't human." For there were brutish faces among those men, lean, yet soft of appearance, and about them hung that thrill of danger, the sensing one has when one meets unexpectedly the snake— there was a great deal more to this group about the old woman than one could gather in one single glance—which was all Derek had time for.

One of the men growled—"Kneel, dog, when you greet the Queen mother. You forced your way in here, may Elnore grant you mercy."

The queen spoke then, gently—absently—"He is strange to our ways, let him stand—'
he will learn manners later."

The man growled—"He'll learn manners later, all right." But the figure on the
throne seemed not to hear the obvious threat of violence to Derek as soon as her back
was turned. Or so Verne's now racing, less-clouded mind sensed in the man's words.

The ray which had driven him here, was now, strangely enough, not burning and
painful, but very caressing upon his shoulder, and the voice in his ear from the ray was
no longer harsh and cruel, but loving and gentle. Derek smelled a strangely dead fish,
but he could not put his finger on it. Why was he treated differently now before this
old ruler?

She spoke again—"Where do you come from? Who are you?"

Derek did not go down on his knee as he perhaps wanted to, but stood, for he was
an American—and they are apt to be that way. He answered—"My name is Derek
Verne. I am the sole survivor of a party of six who set out to find exactly this place—
the dwelling of the Elder Gods—the Elder World, as it has been called. And I found
such an opening as I had hoped existed: I want nothing of you—just to be returned to
the way to the surface, and perhaps some help to open again the way by which I came.
Too, some of my comrades may be alive and hurt under the fall of rock that blocked my
entry way from return, and I request help in seeing that they are found and returned
to their homes, alive or dead. That is all."

The old woman nodded, her face somehow weary. "We will send to see about the
men who were struck and caught by the rocks. The entry way will be opened. About
your return—we will discuss that when you are not here to hear. Our ancient secret is
one that is a wearisome business to guard—an old, old secret, the existence of the
Elder race and its ancient home under the rocks of the surface. To keep the secret, it
would seem you must remain here with us, but we will take counsel upon the matter.

Derek said—"I thank you. I do not understand your ways of life—but I feel a
threat—I do not understand why I should feel fear."

"Do not fear, young man. Nothing will happen to you, except that it may so happen
that you must stay here with us." The ruler Elnore beckoned to a man in a kilt-like
costume who stood stiffly near the entry, and motioned to Derek. Then she went on
stroking the feather fan as though there were no more to be said. Derek followed the
short, thin limbed, grey man at the door, his kilt, the only apparel he wore—was white,
Assyrian in cut. From his belt at his waist hung several strange devices, weapons—
Derek supposed.

Derek asked—after that retreating figure he was following—"What are they going
to do with me? What did the ruler mean when she beckoned you to take me out?"

The man looked at him quizzically. "That ain't the ruler, bud. That's just a minor
character around here, the boss' so-called sister. The boss is even dumber. I never could
figure who really is the boss. It's a mystery, yeh, a mystery! I'm taking you to the
boss."

Another great chamber, another old, vacant-eyed being. This time a man. His eyes
glittered at Derek, his teeth shone like a youth's, his movements were quick and young.
Something unnatural about him—yes, just as the slave had said—something not human.
Yet he looked like a man. But his clothes—they were not of modern times—but then
no one's clothes looked to Derek just as they should look. No one's but his own. This
old man's clothes were like no others Verne had ever seen. From another planet maybe.
They were not woven, seemed to have been poured on his spare figure, shining stuff, silver
like the dress his sister had worn, covered with a fine line decoration that wove strange
alien designs about his limbs, across his chest. His teeth glittered more as he turned
his head, actually smiled at Verne, but there was something fishy—something—Derek
couldn't quite place it—these people despised him, he realized—thought of him as a
lower animal—a nice enough animal but one whose life or death was of no more moment
than a fly. Slowly it came to him. They *lived* in this intoxicating, overwhelming pleasure
of the vibrants manufactured by the great machine in which they lived as in a house—
it was a house—yet still a machine. Here they lived, and something whispered the thought
within his mind—here they lived—*for centuries and centuries!* These clothes are not
alien to this earth—but to your *time!*

These people are not from another planet—they are from an earlier time—these
things about them you notice are the result of centuries of long life—they are old, old—
for within the life-machine people do not die—not for many centuries—time is different

—and they do not care for or have a regard for life outside. They do not even know or understand the modern science of the surface—They have so much pleasure inside this machine—they do not even look up to see if we can be helped or hindered upstairs on the surface. "You are in a strange place, Derek Verne, watch your step." The strange little voice in his mind ceased, and for an instant Derek felt a strange wonderful thrill—it was somehow as though an angel had brushed him with her guardian wing. Someone had given him understanding of this place.

Derek decided not to stand dumb—but to make himself reckoned, heard—to be a man among these—what were they—from the past. "I have been brought here—I come not of my choosing. What is this place? Why I am I here? What do you want of me?" The old man only kept on smiling at Derek, and a ray swept visibly across the room, touched his white head, and now he spoke. "Ah, a visitor from the surface. How came you here?"

Derek explained carefully, just as he had with the old woman in the other throne room. The old man listened, vacant-eyed. The ancient answered in almost the same words his sister had used—

"Do not fear, young man. Nothing will happen to you." Then he beckoned to the guard, just as his sister had done. Again Derek was led away.

Was that the boss?" Derek asked his guard.

"Just another figurehead. They keep them around to look good-goody when certain dangerous visitors are expected. I'm taking you to the real boss of the place.

The guard paused before a great closed door, peered intently for a moment through the crack of the door, then pushed the door open a foot and motioned Derek inside. The guard did not enter. Derek learned why, later.

Now Derek came into the great room, and there were games upon the walls and in one place a great target the size of a man. Hung to the target by four iron pegs, and bracelets hung from the pegs—by her four limbs was a woman, a lovely red-haired creature, her white body struggling in rage with her bonds, her hair a mass of flung red gold about her—and her face, so beautiful—so angry, and so very desperate—resigned, yet struggling—knowing she was as good as dead, yet still fighting for life. Before her stood the man Derek knew at once was responsible for the despair and resigned, desperate hopelessness in the faces of those slaves—in his hands a bunch of large darts. He poised one of the darts in his hands, and looked inquiringly at the girl shackled to the target. She did not even look at him, on her face one could read that of all the ugly sights on earth his face was to her the one most repellant. He poised the heavy, steel pointed dart in his hand, and suddenly with a twisted smile, flung it at the girl, not gracefully—but with a short sharp heave, as though even its pound or two of weight were distasteful to him. She writhed her slim waist aside, the dart cut through her side and hung in her flesh. The blood started trickling down. The man flung another, evidently vexed he had not pierced the heart at the first throw.

\* \* \*

## NOTE TO READER

*Next issue will conclude Mandark and the story of Derek Verne to complete the only extant history of the caverns of the Elder race. Shaver Mystery Magazine has given you the rarest of all writings upon this old globe—for many centuries all such writings have been diligently destroyed by those who keep the caverns secret. For that reason, take care of your copies of Mandark in Shaver Mystery Magazine, for in years to come they will become very, very rare indeed, if the experience of those who have had other accounts of the cavern world is any criterion. It may be that "they" will again attempt to destroy all surface life knowledge of the caverns of the Elder race. It may be that this is the only published account of the true underworld—and it may be that there will be no more for centuries again—who knows? Many difficulties have been overcome to present this account.*

*Shaver*

Follows a dissertation and data on the caves and allied subjects, originally intended as footnote material for Mandark, which was planned to be printed with a split page upper story and lower part, non-fiction. This plan could not be followed due to change.

THE world of wonders that is the Elder world of Caverns contains endless surprises—endless unbelievable things.

But to me the most wonderful, the most deeply interesting, the most horrifying and alien beings, the strangest of all things in the caverns—are those creatures, once men; still men—who have taken up life within a machine.

These machines in which one can live without leaving, are of many kinds. They were originally, I think, healing places where badly injured individuals were placed under perfectly controlled conditions of energy flows, temperature, humidity, etc., so that their bodies would have the best possible chances of recovery.

*FOOTNOTE*:

_____

*In previous issue, the actual chronological account of the Life of Yahveh comes to an end. Mandark continues with dissertation upon the nature and history of the cavern dwellers, and this dissertation lays the floor for a depiction of the modern life in the caverns under Jerusalem. This modern time is described for you in the last part of Mandark, called "Derek Verne"—which is the experiences of an American treasure hunter who stumbles into the former realm of Yahveh and Lila Onderde. This last part of Mandark is begun in this instalment.*

But among some of the older members of the races of the caverns, are some who have inherited the tendency to take up a permanent residence within these machines, never to leave them except for absolute necessity.

Thus they leave behind forever the human characteristic of motion, and become, like the nautilus, the clam, the oyster, a creature which cannot live outside its shell.

But what a shell it is, and how right they are to so take up residence in the most perfect set of living conditions within this world—or on this world.

The machines are built of some perfectly insulating material, a metal impervious to all exterior energy of any kind, and within is a multitude of little ray generators which set up within the impervious metal, a field of fluid force best calculated to support life. Water, treated by certain unknown processes, flows at the press of a button from a nozzle near the mouth—stimulative pleasure rays can be kept on the body for centuries, if desired—and these people who live in these machines *do* so desire—it is their life. Dream records, a library of automatically changing views of the ancient life made up into story form—into plays and phantasmagoria can be continuously made to operate so as to keep the mind of the inhabitant in a continual dream world of wonder unknown to those who have not seen the antique record mech.

Rays from the machines can be sent out to watch the outer world—the world of enemies outside the impervious metal shell of the machine. Inside the artificial world of the dwelling machine, the individual takes up his life of perfection calculated for the complete satisfaction (and development of a cure) (for some injured of the Elder race) —takes up his life and lives on and on in the perfect conditions within the machine for centuries upon centuries.

Within such machines, scattered all over earth, are these individuals—and their numbers, though perhaps few numerically—constitute the greatest power of wisdom on earth. *Yet* they are *not* wholly *human,* they are the product of the past—their minds began their life centuries ago when medievalism was still the way of the surface world.

Many of them, from centuries of such immobile life, have nearly lost the use of their limbs—but the ancient science was of such a nature that they have won something far more powerful than healthy biceps, from constant dreaming of the ancient records of life over and over.

They have won a knowledge of the uses of indescribably powerful and endlessly varied machinery which lies about the cavern, and here and there, (some few of them,) have impressed their control rays and a loyalty upon a group of cavern men—and have for themselves a powerful little group of subjects ready and able to throw all the antique lightning in warfare that the God-race themselves were able to throw—with the machines available—

Such members of the "ancients"—as they are called—the oldest and longest lived of the cavern life—are much feared by the wild nomads—the "rods" or "dero"—those people who wander always through the endless labyrinth of rock borings, under the terrible mental compulsion of hereditary weakness to "de". (De is what the ancients called those forces, those electric fluids of earth's magnetic field which, entering the mind—so rule the thought as to make the mind a "detrimental" an evil, and destructive one. They inherit this tendency from their ancestors—who used the same rays they watched the surface and the other tunnels with—to bring the sunlight down from the surface—by focusing its conductive rays upon the sun. The sun-polared metal, became, after being so used—an agent of sun polarity which eventually made the matter of their minds sun-polared—inductive of these "de" forces—instead of the natural earth-polared matter which inducts the beneficial energies of earth magnetism).

To my knowledge, most of the powerful rulers of the cavern life are of this class—and keep that class pretty strictly to their relatives—but they are fecund because of the nature of the rays—and it may be that most of the cavern life was in the far past descended from the wombs of such "machine dwellers."

But as the livable and untouched portions of the ancient cities become rarer and rarer as time goes on, the facilities for becoming one of these "immortals" (whose age varies between two hundred and five hundred years, so near as I can judge) become more and more scarce—and they are a vanishing phase of the life of the caverns.

For, once a machine has been so used for centuries by such an inhabitant—the whole intricate mechanism becomes worn out and useless—and nothing is more to be dreaded than the conflicts which sometimes arise over new and unused living machines—by those forced to abandon their previous dwelling and look for new quarters as the ancient machines break down from over-use and lack of repair. Then the young-old inhabitant, his limbs atrophied from centuries and more of gazing at the endless and irresistible records of the life of the Elder race, and lying in the insupportably pleasant, the infinite ecstasy, of the stim-rays and the strengthening and invigorating beneficial rays,—his limbs, as I say,—atrophied by lack of exercise,—but grown fat and huge from overgrowth—his great body comes at last out of its shell. His minions are made to rig up a conveyance for him equipped with all the portable pleasure and beneficial ray mech available—and the whole menage—of a hundred or two hundred people—the will-less subjects, the lovely harem of slave girls, the robot warriors whose skill with the long range ray-needles has won them the right to live from the often cruel ruler—all begin their trek to new quarters—sometimes chosen beforehand and sometimes to be found only after long pilgrimages through the ever-perilous dark.

Now he comes at last to an undestroyed and inhabitable portion of the caves, where there is no water, no damp, the air is warm and dry and fresh—the machines are untouched by corrosion—and to his knowledge not too-long used by others of his kind.

If some other inhabitant has taken up his ruler-life in a living machine—he carefully sends out his scouts, sounds out their strength and knowledge of the antique weapons, and if they appear quite ignorant and foolish, the war for possession of the area begins. This fight is usually horrible for this reason:

The incomer is usually an old crab from long exposure to an aging mech—in residence in the machine. He is not of our modern age—but of an age when they had as daily occurrences the burning of witches—the torture of innocents—the horrors of medievalism. He is also a victim of his ignorance, for all machinery of the caverns—that is, the kind that make the rays necessary to all life in the dark—(the rays that take the place of the beneficial actinic rays of the sun)—suffer from that physical ailment of radio-activity from which the Elder race fled so long ago. (The ailment which they called "de"—which can best be described to you by the words—"Sun-polarity"—an affliction of all electrical materials used under a sun—so that they become more and more sun-inductive as their use goes on—so that they become more and more detrimental generators of "de" as the centuries pass and this "de" polarity of the metal is conducted by the nature of the rays to the body of the subject—who becomes in time sun-polared too—and sun-polared minds are "evil" minds.)

Now the person whom he decides to attack in order to appropriate his less used and less long-inhabited quarters for himself—to continue his centuries old but now evil life—this person is of necessity younger and less able to defend himself—this inexperience and youth probably only a century or so of age—being his weak point but also his strength in that this younger inhabitant of the life machines does not have his body so badly under the influence of the evil-nature-causing sun-polarity from the aging machines.

So it is that all "good" or earth-polared young people of the caverns who are in a position to defend and expand and develop the wonders of the super-technical ancient civilization—are in constant fear and hiding from these relics of the past—the inevitably evil, irrascible, and hereditarily tyrannical "chamber-dwellers" of a cunning enhanced by centuries of experience and the stuff of the records and writings of the Elder race—

though—being medieval-minded to begin with they have no such ideals or plans for the education and development of the race of man.—(Which is a rather modern idea—a development of the last few centuries of life on the surface—and never a generally held ideal of the cavern life.)

So it is that we have in the caverns a young and inexperienced group of people who must defend themselves and all men's future against ancient tyrannical over-lords who believe only in complete subjugation of the people about them to ray-control—a kind of robot life—under their own complete mental domination.

The younger, from watching surface life—listening over their unseen rays to our college professors—(and laughing frequently at the professor's innocence and lack of knowledge of the truths of life) have acquired some of the ideals and goals of general education—they love people, plan ahead for their young, have schools (did you ever hear of the "Deep" schools?) and in general are an entirely different lot than their older predecessors.

But they have this terrible enemy, a wily, cunning "old man of the sea," who may come out of the endless dark labyrinth of the far tunnels at any time and kill them all before they even know he is present. For his age of life with the terrible and endless mystery of the caverns has given him knowledge of the varied machines and weapons which make him an invincible antagonist—and he sometimes knows enough about physics and the ailments of the life-ray mech that he knows he must move his residence every few years in order to have fresh and un-sun-polared—"un-de" mech, so that his beneficial rays, which are responsible for his long and often terrible life will keep him alive.

When this "old man of the sea" knows that much about life and the ray mech, he also knows plenty about the terrible and varied uses of the infinitely powerful weapons of the ancients, and has had centuries of exploration of the endless reaches of the caverns to find and bring to himself those weapons most apt to prove disastrous to a young and untried enemy.

So the war-fare of the caverns is ever a fight between idealist, liberal youth, vs. terrible and tyrannical, cruel and dotard age.

Around these battles of the old and the young "immortals" of the cavern life, are ever the "dough", the people of the caverns, their thin white limbs, their stooped underfed bodies, their faces which reflect the sorrows of ages of subjection to tyranny and the wrong life-conditions which are theirs when they are denied access to these rays which life must have to be healthy life in the caverns. Too, they have not always the best medical care in the world, and their food supply is poor, being subject ever to the whims of those who make of the few and secret entrances a port of entry for food which is priced by their greed for values—values such as pretty slaves, powerful stim mech, and the other rarities of the cavern life—values far beyond what we of the surface know as values.

These sorrowful slaves to the rulers of the entries, to the rulers who live for centuries within the life-mech, subjected to the infinite pleasures of lifetimes of stim-rays, pleasures which can be described only inadequately as "infinite ecstasy" but which your ignorance of the nature of stim cannot imagine as the terrific and irresistible flood of delight of infinitely seductive and voluptuous delight such as no man not of the caverns can begin to picture, a thing as alien to surface life as wine from the vintners of Mars. These slaves to the rulers do the work, and take the beatings, the indignities, the sadistic torturings. The endlessly subjugating work of people who have an age of such traditions behind them to tell the rulers what to do to make their people wholly slaves to their will. —They take it all hopelessly because there is no way to get back at a man within such a life-machine—a man with centuries of wisdom in the ways of life where themselves have but twenty or so years of misery in their mind with which to struggle against this invincible opponent. So they are subject—to misery.

Around them is another terrible ring of fear, (their nucleus being this "immortal" within his life machine for whom they work and die) around them is another thing they fear and hate—the "rods", the terrible dero of the caverns—the nomads whose life span, though short, is dreadful to all it contacts for they do not know any mental reaction but "fear" and "fight"—like Indians against the pioneers, to see is to try to kill—they hate those who live in groups, who preserve any semblance of civilization or sense or kindliness—they are a kind of demon, whose use of ray-mech for pleasure which the wise of the caverns would never touch—has resulted in hereditary weakness for the sun-polarity of the mind which is "evil"—which is the "rod" the "dero" the dread native of the caves who has sunk into a savagery of desperation and privation such as surface life cannot visualize till it sees it. They live upon the white lizards, the blind fish of the few streams of the caves, upon certain dark dwelling insects—and upon each other, upon a few places in the caverns where the entries to the surface are not held by rulers, where they can shoot game with their rays and go out and bring it in to the darkness during the night.— That night—that dark to us—is to them so very bright they can hardly bear to enter it— hardly bear the brightness of the pitch black night. They have large eyes, accustomed for an age to absolute blackness—can see dimly even in this darkness—and at night go to the surface and hunt—or hunt through the caves for humans, unaware, to eat.—These are the "rods"—whom they fear, a degenerate form of man, a demon in truth, and the source of our demon legends. Around these communities who serve such rulers are always the "rods" awaiting a chance to grab off a fat child, a woman to play with before they eat her—and there is no more fearful creature to encounter, as some mad-men of the surface can tell you with their gibbering.

So it is they cannot leave their master in the life-machine for his long range rays, which the lowlier dare not touch, protect them all from raids by these dero, and so it is they are always between the devils and the dark master within his life-machine.

But here and there the young idealists, and their sane, older members hold forth, and these are the spots all these oppressed dream of, sing of in their sorrowful songs, hope sometime to reach in some way. These are the "heavens to which they look forward"—their only hope—to find at least a kind master within a life-machine who will appreciate and properly reward their work, and not make mindless slaves of them by merciless cutting of their minds so that they will serve without question or pay for the rest of their poor lives. But, you say, why don't these powerful and long lived people come to the surface and rule as they seem so able to do?

Because the clam or the nautilus does not come out of the sea and chase birds through the trees. It is not natural to them, the machines which support their long and alien life are neither available on the surface nor are they portable to the surface—and their life—a half dream from constant use of the ancient thought records for entertainment—a vast, superior sort of entertainment which can only be described to you—never *conveyed* to you in its entirety as the most terrific experience possible on this earth—has made them cynical of ever obtaining anything better—scornful of all life that does not measure up to the impossible standard of the antique wonder-race.—The life which they lead during their playing of these records—of which there is a vast supply—is so superior they do not care for what we have to offer on the surface.—Their whole aim in life is to make their existence (in the dreamstate in which these records are experienced just as life is experienced—only more intensely by far)—safe!—To make that existence self-supporting and safe from marauders who would steal their location and their wonder-mech from them. That is the greatest visible value—and just as game congregates and lives within reach of the water hole—just as the earthworms grow best in the richest ground—so do they confine their expansion to those areas of the caverns which are in such a good condition as to make their age-old way of life possible to them. It is an alien and wonderful kind of life—and their bodies and natures are alien and strange to us of the surface. One cannot say they are not normal, or that we are normal—we are products of a way of life totally different in every one of its conditions from theirs, (and by "conditions" I mean vastly more than is usually conveyed by the word—I mean inductive and penetrative energy flows around us—synthetic from the hand of the dead Elder race in their case.—In our case—the product of nature and the sun.—In their case their food and water are second in importance to their acquisition of these wonder health rays of the antique manufacture.—In our case "food and water" constitute almost the whole of what we mean by "conditions of life"—)

Their food is often wholly from the vast stores of sealed containers of food left behind by the departing Elder race in their haste to flee from the nearing and deadly sun which had captured earth from out its orbit through dark space.—(And for good reason —for upon its first approach to the sun, the earth came so near as to burn off from its surface every trace of the life of these vast bodied and infinitely wise Elder race—the buildings they had erected over the ever-ice of the cold planet—the great entry locks by which they entered their cavern cities—the vast railroad systems that spanned the endless areas of ice and linked the whole surface in a great network of metal—the sun destroyed it all and heated the whole surface of earth to incandescence—and that is why we, even today—do not know what is meant by the word "God"—but visualize some great cloud body—omniscient, omnipresent, and quite impossible of visualization as no man can know enough to visualize the truth of such a super-being. The Gods were a race of vast power and beauty, true—but they were material flesh and blood like ourselves, and though their bodies varied they were many of them of like appearance to ourselves.

The nectar and ambrosia (of the latter legendary grecian Gods) was this same food of the Gods—stored for an age in the sealed compartments of their great metal dwellings within the caverns—it is still useable today—though these stores of food grow rarer.

As most of the great dwellings are entirely too large for modernized humans comfort, there have been built, around the machine dwellers houses of wood and plaster, very like surface buildings, often by men from the surface—men "impressed" for the job,— (stolen from their surface homes by one dodge or another)—Filled with second-hand furniture—(at least it looks today like the antiques we see in second-hand stores,) as the inflow of goods from the surface is necessarily limited by the guarding secrecy which has always been the main feature of their contact with the surface.—To see these streets of dwellings along the ancient caverns, under the loom of the vast statues of the Elder race,—along the railway, now unused, that once spanned the continent, now lies forever deserted of its natural traffic,—to see these buildings, looking like a street taken from the "Nineties" of surface life—filled with the outmoded furniture of the bygone centuries —*still used* by the people of the caverns is very strange! New dwellings are built— new stores for their commodities—but still the alien flavor of the life of the cavern remains.—Side by side with a thin man from the cavern clad in slacks and sports coat, one is apt to see a "witch" of the past—clinging still to the tall conical hat, the pointed shoes, the long clinging skirts of her ancestors in England—for antiquity is ever the flavor of the caves. Where did she find such clothes? Perhaps she acquired them from an abandoned dwelling, for the hot dry air of the caves preserves nearly anything exactly as it is left. More like her mothers, and her mothers before her—were made the same. (There are few insects.)

Next to a log cabin, still standing, one finds a house built of split lumber with the adze marks still on it, and beside that a modern frame shack, and beside that a wooden ginger-bread structure of fifty years ago. Within the house one is apt to find the split log bench side by side with the modern chrome tubing chair. And on the wall some of the gleaming fabrics which the Gods alone could weave. And over the whole house looms the mighty elder work, vast bas-reliefs in the walls of the caverns, great metal enigmas stretching up and up, and those stairways, once escalators but now only to be climbed laboriously on foot—laborious not only for their endless height, but because the steps are two feet high.

In writing this book, I have constantly been hampered by the thought that fiction was not the vehicle to tell such a terrific revision of both accepted history and accepted theological beliefs as to the past. I have constantly felt that I should drop the fictional skeleton upon which I had to hang the great, revolutionary truths—and get down to plain brass tacks and say what I meant about all this underworld of the Elder race and the part it has played in the life of the human race. I have felt that if I did so, just wrote as well as I could exactly all I knew about the subject, without invention of characters and incident suitable to tell the vast history of these caverns and of the men who have lived in them since the elder race left, I would have a successful book and a book better understood. So I have compromised and put a story upon the upper parts of the page and the more bald and open notes, or deductive truths of the past "as it must have been" to my mind—and allowed the reader to take his choice as to which to read—or both— as the student who understands will do.

At the time of Christ, the worship of Satan, or something extremely similar was already widespread and very, very old in the caverns, just as it was in the upper world. Some writers try to say that Satan was an invention, a growth that fastened upon the Christian church *after* Christ, but there are entirely too many evidences otherwise. The Pagan Saternalia and the Demoniac Sabbath are obviously quite closely related; however far apart the Christian worship of God is from pagan worship. The utter prostration of the will to an evil principle was perhaps not so terrible and so widespread as it evidently grew to be under the Christian church's frantic witchburning, but this prostration, the utter giving-up-of-the-self to an evil principle, was perhaps never as utter an evil as the witch-burners made out in their endless accounts, (such as Sprenger's) of their trials and tortures of witches and sorcerers.

But this surface world of man is entirely a different place than the underworld, and its life is an entirely different thing, and to judge one by the other, or to expect similar behaviour of one because such is the case of the other, is entirely the wrong way to think of the history of the caverns. For in the caverns, very special and greatly variant conditions held forth. Some of the vast cities were built at different times from others, and the machinery of life that has made them livable for so long was perhaps exhausted and abandoned long before the Elder race abandoned earth under the fiery breath of the approaching sun—or change of the sun—which did eventually drive them from this part of space forever, and would so drive us if we had sense and power to go.

In some places in the endless, wonder-warrens there were machines that gave forth endlessly flows of light and warmth, that made great gardens bloom, that made living there very healthy. There the Latter Gods developed into a pale echo of the Elder race. An echo only, it is true; but still not evil people.

These favorable places have continued to be found in the caverns down to the present day, and there have always been the "good people"—"the mysterious helpers" who have sought to help surface man with the magic of the wonder machines of the Gods.

In other places, the same original sources of race have been subjected to gradually deteriorating flows of the energy from the life-machines, have used stim mech which were worn out before they ever got hold of them—and there conditions of life were vastly different than in the favorable places. There developed another kind of man, not like man at all—and these minds were pre-disposed by the nature of the artificial conditions of life to a weakness for evil thought. Born in the half-dark, subjected all their life to a weak beneficial ray from a worn-out machine which did not succeed in making the deep cavern a place for life to grow at all—still they lived—and became the horrors that some man-life in the caverns still is today. Thin, white-bodied, like potato shoots in the dark cellar are compared to potato plants in the sun—so did they compare in appearance to normal man—a different kind of thing entirely from normal surface man—just as the people of the good places are a different kind of thing than surface man entirely, but in the opposite way. All the good qualities they may have inherited from their parents turned under these terrible degenerating machine rays into the opposite of normal life, into evil. And the elder race explained the nature of evil to us forever by making the spelling of *evil* the backward from *live*. It *is* backward, believe me! Still, equipped with the terrible machines, they have managed to make their way of life survive, even until today—and still today they keep the secrecy that has protected their singular appearance from men of the surface. Also they have kept their private hells from man's knowledge.

After the death of Christ, after the subjugation of Yahveh to the Evil Lila, (which you can consider symbolically or as you wish, although it is the actual tale as the lore of the caverns holds it to have happened—after the growth of evil rule under the impetus of the evil queen who enslaved the mind of the Messiah for all his life—

Satanism became a general condition, the government over a large part of the caverns under Europe. The tales of surface man all through the dark and middle ages show this to have been the case—show the ideology of the underworld. It is expressed everywhere that the writings of surface man show contact with the underworld to have been primarily satanism,—Satanic. The demons, the demon "lovers," the imps of satan— the witches—the whole dark ideology and the whole preoccupation of the dark ages the medieval age—with such subjects, show that the underworld was at work with just these types of projections, that medieval man *did* see the Devil's transparent form, *did* see demons with horns, etc., etc., and *did* see witches riding brooms in the sky—

In the pagan past he did *not* see these things, for the thought of underworld men was different—he saw instead the Errinyes, the Furies, he saw Zeus throwing his thunderbolts—he saw Pluto—he saw the river Styx and Charon—he saw the Elysian fields of some vast garden—(a favorable place of the caves, remembered by the underworld from their own legends—or still existent and seen over the ray conductors as truth by surface man). He saw those things of which they both (upper and lower people) thought. The jealous God of the Jews, who had followed them into Egypt and licked the whole Egyptian (Note—I wonder if "Upper and Lower Egypt meant the Nile—or the caves?) underworld to free the Jews from Pharaoh—this jealous, indomitable God so careless and angry—the figure we know as the God of the old testament,—has changed—but the Demon, the Furies—they have not changed—they have become worse.—They are no longer, as they were in the pagan religion, an instrument of punishment which was ruled and guided by the justice of a Pluto or a Zeus or a Jupiter.—No, the demon has become a God in his own right, a god paramount or striving to be a paramount—no longer the instrument of the Good God's vengeance he is now a God who demands the soul from a man, that he may use both the soul and the body to promote the wholesale spread of Evil as way of life.—He gives rewards for evil deeds, for the spreading of plagues he has special rewards, etc. etc. And the Saternalia is not alone a place where one throws off restraint, it becomes a place where the buttocks of the Paramount Demon must be kissed, and where most of the copulation is accomplished by the Devil himself in rewarding his witches who have managed to make all good men miserable. This deluge of evil came after the death of Christ on the cross—for before then enough of humanity remained in the people of the underworld, even the worst, that they did not think entirely backwards—as the increasing flows of disintegrant energy from the worn old ray mech was making them do now.

So it was that the welfare of man on the surface became the especial goal of all the deviltry the underworld could concept—and the Dance of Death, the time of the Great Plagues—were the result of this striving to destroy men.

We can tell from the universal use of the "witches doll" that many of the underworld had by this time lost all power of speech, for the witches found no way to communicate their demands and wishes to them, but by the construction of a doll resembling the object of their hate, and when the witch wanted the person hurt, she plunged a pin into the doll, and the underworld, understanding that the witch wanted the person hurt—plunged his long ray beam up through the rock and into the victim, who shrieked and died.—(Or was put away in the pest house for one bewitched.) But the evil little potato sprout of a man, white and shrunken and no longer even human in appearance, was not "believed in" except as an invisible "spirit". It is sad that that condition still holds true today. But it is encouraging that the witch's doll, and the underworld obliging her (the witch), are so infrequent today.

But all that past history of life in the caverns, so pitiful and yet so wonderful, so terrible in its utter loss of the natural human rights of man to a thing that cannot even be dignified with the name Evil, for it has also lost all intelligence—and all that past history of the Godlike beings of the caverns, dwelling in the specially favored areas of the caverns, trying always to "save" man and not understanding that he can only be saved by studying and copying the machines and methods that have given them their special conditions of life.—Not profoundly educated or habituated to study, leading a lazy life of luxury in their easily conquered special life conditions, fighting the evil of the caverns only when it threatened their own lives and areas—waiting always for the return of the Elder race and the wonderful God of the Elder races who was going to make everything right everywhere all over the earth—never understanding that earth can never be well and free of evil so long as disintegrant electric induction from the sun makes of the weaker brains an instrument of detrimental power—never quite realizing their duty to themselves and others. All that history of the conflict of these two kinds of special creatures of the caverns, whose works are best recognized—whose natures are best understood, when we realize that the better kind of people of the caverns gave rise to the legends of the "little people" or "the Fairies"—while the evil of the caverns gave rise to legends of "the Devil" and his "Hell" in the "Underworld" must be more or less reconstructed after the manner in which Dinosaurs are re-constructed by our pundits of the past—and will not be touched by them even when they know, for fear of the disapproval of those moderns who hold that all the past is worthless and only modern science knows anything—and hold up the creation of the "atomic bomb as proof that the past knew nothing" although that same creation has placed all mankind in greater jeopardy than all the evil of the caverns ever was able to place him. (And if certain groups of evil ones in the caverns start building the atomic bombs we have so obligingly created for evil they will have that power they love so well over all men. And there will be no holding them back, for no atomic bomb can reach them in the depths where their homes are. And that may happen, that they will come out and erase from earth the hated "men"—"meat men"—who are so big and tanned and healthy, and then their pale dwarfed children will inherit all the earth).

For in truth only the bare bones are left of the history of the caverns since they were abandoned so very long ago. That nearer past is harder to come by than the past of the Elder race itself, for that is shielded and protected by the very machinery and chambers and blanket of grey dust a foot thick, and by the very fact of the eternal bigness of the caverns, which are so surfaced in area by the many levels in which they bored that the total floor area of the caverns is many, many times the surface area of earth! It is a much bigger world than the surface, and all the centuries of life in it by the hiding wights who have kept it secret have not been able to touch a great part of it yet.

And the traces of the centuries that have passed since the Elder race left are but scratches upon the great cavern record of their life—the great Elder race. But both are there to be read by the modern explorer who dares to think and look.

But both are not to be read by such as our learned psychiatrists, psychologists and singular falsely scientific gentlemen, reveling in the universal explanation for the universal illness—I will quote a few of them on the subject of "demonomanias." Explaining all contacts with the underworld—(which are really necessarily mental and by means of the antique ray—)

*"The possessed persecution maniac carries within himself the Devil, he is at once his dwelling place and his slave. He must submit to his whims, and act according to his direction solely. The Demon speaks through the mouth of the sufferer, thinks with his brain, and acts with his limbs. The "Delusion" of persecution with possession must be distinguished from the analogous confusional and hysterical states described above, and also from delusional anxiety—melancholia. The delusions of the possessed persecution maniac is chronic."*

*". . . . . . Its principle symptom is hallucination. Voices do not come from without, but from within. They speak in the brain, in the tongue, in the heart, in the abdomen; they are various and multiple, uttered with terrifying force . . . . ."*

*"The voices mock, curse and command. The sufferer has the feeling that he possesses a multiple personality. He is astonished by ideas which cross his mind but which are opposed to his normal feelings. Only the Demon can have suggested them (he thinks).*

*"Disorders of both the general and the genital sensibility are very frequent. The patient feels burns, bites, pricks, tearing apart of his limbs, contractions and burning contacts, every variety of violence and violation. Hot or cold breaths pass over his face, mysterious cuppings empty him.*

*"Hallucinations of smell and taste—the smell and taste of sulphur, of faecal matter—complete the picture."*

*(From the "Devil" by Maurice Garcon and Jean Vinchon—from a trans. by Stephen Gaden Guest—orig. pub. in France—and E. P. Dutton—Edition of 1930.)*

This is typical of the picture the learned medicos and students who follow the academic patterns set for these phenomena. *These phenomena are world-wide,* have occurred since ancient times nearly everywhere, and *each of you readers* have known someone who swears they "saw" the devil, or "saw" a witch or some such fly-by-night, so-called "hallucination". The medicos know very well, if they know anything, that there is a great deal more to such things than mere "hallucination" for it is odd that the *same* hallucinations, even down to *minutest detail,* should survive so many centuries, so generally!

In the same book they confute this stand against acceptance of the reality of the Demon—a very worthy stand, you must admit—to refuse to credit with reality what is so general and so terrible—for the sake of saving the minds of their so generally mad brethren and citizens—but *nevertheless* a stand that distorts the truth to achieve a desired end! It is the stand many who knew better took in medieval times to halt the widespread persecution and burning of the afflicted. So it is excused today, except for the fact the same attitude is used by medicos to fill our mad-houses with quite sane people who have had "hallucinations".

A paragraph in the same book *refutes* this very contention they uphold, that all these "hallucinations" are purely madness. Here is the paragraph by the same pair of authors.

"If they regard as mad a man who believes in the Devil, they have to arrive at this conclusion—that for centuries entire peoples and diverse civilizations were composed only of the mad! This paradox cannot be sustained."

So I must hurl this paragraph in the teeth of all who contend that "hallucinations of this type are had only by the mad". I must say too, that "everyone who believes in the existence of God is *not* mad or else whole peoples, whole civilizations of the past have been mad." So it is that we cannot accept that our learned medical frauds and pundits are right, who hold that all such phenomena are purely the product of disordered minds, for such phenomena have been entirely too generally experienced and believed in—up to the point where billions of people, extending from the first Egyptian pyramid down through time to the present day—have held these apparitions are real and that they come from the underworld.

That antique stand is taken by myself today, from a thorough knowledge of both the underworld and its people, and I say these modern medicos who hold that all "demonomanias", and persecution "complexes", are "delusions based upon imagination and disorders of the imagination." That all this learned crew are but throwing sand in our eyes because they know and fear the truth—or simply because they fear to uphold the truth because it is not the fashion just now to hold that phantoms have a genuine and marvelous cause—*outside* the brain of the afflicted. If it were the fashion, as it was in the middle ages, to attribute all this night witchery to the devil and his imps, these same learned psychologists and psychiatrists would be the first to swing to the new fashion, in order not to be otherwise than the "accepted." These psychologists would swear the devil rode their bedpost every night, if it would be fashionable so to do! But the truth of things is not arrived at that way. We must hold opinions for considered and logical reasons, and not because they are the fashion. It is the fashion at present to attribute all such weird phenomena to the disorders of the mind, and to have the man psycho-analyzed, etc.

But the truth is—all this is a cowardly glossing over of the terrible truth, which is that earth and its people suffer from a terrible thing they cannot understand, and have so suffered for ages.

The truth is that the caverns under our feet *are* full of vast mysterious machines, and the caverns *are* full of peculiar people who have inherited the custom of doing their mad will with "our" minds by means of these machines, and all the learned explanations to the contrary, that is the *truth* of the matter! Those people who feel bites, burns, pricks, and tearing of the limbs, who feel their blood drained away from them, who are lifted strangely into the air and left there for long periods, who see in the night six-foot spiders with women's heads, who have things strangely like medieval succubi and incubi cohabit with them awake and in their sleep, these people who are "followed" continually for long periods by a strange "invisible" tormenting being—those people like De Maupassant when he tells his own experiences in the story "The Horla"—all these people, stretching back through hoary time so far as the written word reaches and far beyond in the folk tales of man—all these people were NOT HAVING HALLUCINA-TIONS! They were for the most part *telling the truth* and being very careful not to embroider it! All those marvelous things, for the most part, all those agonies of the mind and body from mysterious beings were *truly experiences* by means of the rays *from underneath*—and man has been too stupid to know what a ray is and how a ray works. He still is too stupid, and when a man or woman goes to the FBI with a tale of being tormented by "Radio waves which read his thought and give him other hard-to-bear thoughts, of being burned by these radio waves, etc." putting all the familiar old phenomena into modern terminology—they do not listen to the familiar tale without having the same old reactions, "The bird is nuts, poor guy."

But here was added injury to insult, for frequently his freedom is taken, he is shut up in the madhouse—he has "hallucinations". (true enough.) But so have had all people everywhere, so long as history was written, "seen the devil," felt his burning and his pricking, and so he does today, but today it is called "radio waves". *It is the same old witchcraft,* and it goes on today— !—

But down below in the endless caverns, down there is no law, and the poor white, thin little potato-shoot men and women have nothing better to do than torment us, nor have they inherited better minds than minds that tell them to do little else but find food. And finding food is a job down there, for the entrances are guarded by the same old repressive families who charge a terrible tax for all that enters the underworld.

These gray little people who cause these delusions and persecutions, are not entirely to blame for their acts. They are the product of a long age of persecution themselves, by those who hold the entrances to the underworld, who live in an endless profusion of luxury and parasitism upon surface man and upon their worst victim, the men of the underworld. They (the rulers?) have little mind left, or will either, to do aught but play with the antique wonder machinery that stands about everywhere down there, neglected and covered with a foot of grey dust, yet still obedient to the touch of a hand upon its buttons and levers. (For the Elder race did not build to a central power plant as we do—but powered each unit separately with its own power source—and these, perhaps the most important of the ancient works, are still used to give forth tremendous flows of energy for ray-making, for the levitation beams used, etc.)

Typical clip from my notebooks. You can find such items every day in some newspaper from some part of the world. I would suggest club members keep such clips or mail them in— eventually to be made into one more volume of inescapable evidence of the truth.

## THE MANDRIL'S HANDS

When they found the hands, they said they were the hands of a woman. As I recall, they found them stuck on the pickets of an iron fence, like gloves set out to dry.

For a couple of days the police were looking for the body of a woman.

Then they announced that the hands were non-human, since the prints were such as are found on no human beings finger tips, being cross wise instead of round and round.

Now for a day or two the police are looking for a woman's body who is not human! To match hands which are like woman's hands but are not a woman's hands they are looking, looking for a body!

Now comes the paper with a picture of a mandril, a big ape that runs on all fours— and they say the hands are from that ape, are that kind of hands.

You cannot blame the police if they could not find a dead woman's body to match the hands of a mandril, who is well known for sincerely murderous ability, as well as walking on his hands. We have very few women who walk on their hands.

What interests me most is the picture of the joker who went to the zoo's grave yard, dug up the dead mandril, cut off the hands, reburied the ape, and then placed the hands on a picket fence for the embarassment of the police. Such a joker should be on the radio or the movies.

## LIFE OF FATAL AUTO CRASH DRIVER RULED BY 'LITTLE MEN'

A weird story of little men who tried to govern the life of Lester A. Ulberg, 30, San Diego advertising salesman, was unfolded at an inquest yesterday into his death during a "ride to heaven" auto crash.

Ulberg was killed instantly June 17 when, according to hitch-hiking passengers, he drove his auto into a loaded hay truck on Highway 80, near Descanso, after telling them, "I'm going to take you all the way—all the way to heaven."

An eight-man coroner's jury found Ulberg came to his death by driving the machine into the truck while temporarily insane.

The passengers, Bruce T. Pegg, 20, and Ross Williams, 23, of San Diego, escaped serious injury. They said they had ridden about three miles with Ulberg.

They were en route to Las Vegas for a short yacation before starting a new semester at San Diego State College.

Ernest George Epplar, of 3930 First Ave., associated with Ulberg in an advertising campaign, told the jury he spent several hours with Ulberg the night of the accident.

He related that Ulberg had been "very nervous and moody." Then he told of his strange actions during a 10-day period they had been associated.

"He had a lot of weird ideas about life. He seemed quite anxious about his past. He didn't mention anything in particular but said he wished he had never done some of the things he did.

"Les talked a lot about little men," Epplar said. "He showed me a room where he said he used to go to think. He used to practice Yoga there. 'Sometimes while he was in the room' he told me, 'little men standing on the bed would tell him what to do, some of them were good and some were evil,' he would say."

Epplar reported Ulberg had a lot of bills and financial worries. Pegg and Williams testified Ulberg acted "strangely."

"He talked a lot about a music program that was playing. He talked in a dull monotone and seemed to repeat everything twice," Pegg, sitting next to him, reported. "He said several times he would take us all the way. Then, as we went over a little hill, he began edging toward a truck. Just before we got to it, he added, 'you are going all the way to heaven.' The crash came in a matter of seconds."

Williams corroborated the testimony, adding that he had tried to avert the crash by grabbing the steering wheel but had been unsuccessful in missing the truck.

Other witnesses were John Williams, of Alpine, driver of the hay truck, who reported he tried to avoid the accident by pulling over as far as possible to the side of the road; Highway Patrolman George A. Dowdy, Alton H. Rogers, employment agency operator, who knew Ulberg; Andrew Kitzman, owner of the plumbing concern, for which Ulberg worker, and Ulberg's widow.

OF EROS
*or*

Is this, then, Verse? No, just thought, Reader. If you don't like verse in **your Club**
Magazine, let us know, for it is being sent quite often.

FAINT and far beats the still sweep of the Now.
    O, give relief from all the burning future
    While in the fleeing is a hard, cool dread.
Flaming to fearful birth.
"Strike the still charm ringing silent—Silence!
In the night, strike the metal—
Strike the flesh with rose
And the rock with piercing cries
Fling the false after
Say all the words that were "best unsaid"
Speak out all the shame of truth
When all men desire instead a "faery" lie!
Flop wings of bat-leather
Or pinions of rainbow glory—
Above the cauldron's breath—
Bear into the mornings freshness
The stench of the lie in the night.
Hear the concealers shriek—
"Thou! It is thou who told the light!
Told that in the night is hidden
What "cannot be," and "is not"
Except for the Eye of Reality!"
Hear yet other shrieks—
"The sweet breast of truth
Is pierced, now, and the read flame of her blood
Spread for all to see!
What crime is yours, O butcher?
To say what is NEVER SAID?"
Or hear—"Not even evil, not the devil
Not any servant of sin, ever
Managed such crime as this—
*To speak of the unspoken!*
News from the barriers that "are not"
Word from the womb of night—
Word of the birth of the future
That word that "Must never be said!"
"Thou hast said it, even thou!
Thou accursed and unwanted—
Thou cast our servant of our Master—
Thou last least lees of sin's cup!"
Hear—
You have broken the seal of the lie!
You have shown men their grave—
**You have spoken to the meat-things of their slaughter!**
You have revealed to the virgin her unconscious rape—
To even children you have shown
The bodies of their parents!
It is sad they should know.
They are things that must not know.
They must never see the dead sad face of life—
To flit their brief life away
Is for them the truth, NOT the awful face of effort!
But only the dull plodding of the beast for them!
Not the courageous leap at the barriers—
NOT THAT FOR THEM!"
"Not for them"—said the thing of the night.
"Only death and ignorance can be theirs—

I have said it—the Lords have said it—
It is the ancient word of the law!
*It Must be!"*
I listened as one listens to all ghosts
With but a deaf ear. I spoke out—

I said the fearful words!
And the world whirled on,
Nor stopped aghast!
So speak on and on,
Nor ever hear the fear in the night that may not—
Nor the baying of the hound that is not even dog.

Form, life's shaped beauty,
Vigorous pulsing fecundity . . .
These are for you the Lord you serve,
And not the secretive silence in the night
That fears to be!
Life is the child you care for and the woman you worship!

Wisdom, clean pure truth, understandable
Shaped mildly to the true mans head—
These are your work.
The nights dark wizardry of lust,
The crawling brazenness of sun-lights sin,
The cruelly blinding poison of evil writings,

Designed to put out forever all logic
And all truth on earth—
*These* are your enemies!
The false shouting of stupidity
The fearful prostration before the fearful phantasm—
The little ones calling God—

The timid suppression of natural fecund pleasure—
The crimes endlessly repeated against Love and Thought—
All these are your enemies
And you must fight on!
The weakening of your "will"
The dull stupidity darkening your mind—
The fear of others blindness failing to use
The Elder formulae for simple truth in thought—
The failure of others to make effort
And only your own loneliness striving—
These are your false barriers—
Or true barriers, what is the difference—
Climb them you must!
You serve the youth of the future—you who read and know—
You must serve him well,
He has not wronged you, nor will he!
The futile repetitions forced upon you—
The reactions to faked stimulae given you—
Love troubled and split away—
Wars and hatred and strife multiplied—
Imitations of life forever pictured—
Called "writing"—even I must do it to you—
When the thought leads another path toward truth!
That other thing—why does it shape into words flaming,
True, and all-conquering?
I will describe your enemy bit by bit—
Where he turns and burns within his evil hiding place.
He is an anger, an ancient hurt, a mutilation of self—
Inverted, terrible, and inhuman.
He is a terrible and an eager sadism,
"Tremendous", inverted being—

Yet a small, despicable, crawling, fearful,
Spiteful, stupidity on legs!
That thing is less than a beast—
Yet more than a man in power for destruction!
Zealot, fanatic, madman—they will call you—
For fighting this thing that burns forever
In its ancient hiding place.
Crusader—Is a crusader, then, one
Who defends himself against a monster as best he can?
He is—when he must fight for all of you—
"There is no monster, sweet people"—
"All is kindness and sweetly charitable beings,
All working for you—and you—and you—"
Is what the thing in the night says—
To those who help his hiding
With their unseeing veiling of his hated body.
Aware, now, of your enemie—
Aware, the future must not die unborn!

---

## NORTH CAROLINA "HORLA" VICTIM

*This account by Red Buck Bryant is typical of the mental state and reactions of men and women persecuted by under-world ray. They are sure it is surface people, and the whole thing is to them an impossible but true thing that happens to them, for which they can get no help and less understanding. Note the device, mysterious to him, that he calls the "Fortune Wheel." It is the telaug. Note that he received no help, but did ask every public official he could contact. It is impossible for such people to understand that prominent surface people are as much mystified as themselves—and in quite as great fear of meeting the same fate if they attempt "investigation".—Editor.*

### RED BUCK BRYANT'S REMINISCENCES
#### By H. E. C. (Red Buck) Bryant
#### (Matthews, N. C., R. F. D. No. 1.)

Since I commenced to write reminiscences for The Charlotte Observer I have had hundreds of letters, some of them bouquets, others brickbats, but the strangest one came in response to a story on ghosts or haunts.

The author of it asked that I not use his name if I wrote anything about it. After that I had two other communications from him. At first I thought I would just dismiss the matter from my mind but now for readers who like a puzzle, or a mystery, I have decided to give the substance of the epistles, evidently written by a well-educated person. To keep faith with my correspondent I shall not mention places referred to, because if I did it would be absurd not to identify him.

"If you would like to secure material for an article that really has no precedent or parallel in American history, you might be sufficiently interested to investigate the following," the first letter said.

"On or about the first of July, 1941, while I was serving my government in a job I had had for 11 years, in eastern North Carolina, living in my home in a county seat there, I was secretly hypnotized by a person who operated there under the assumed name of 'Adolph Hitler,' who uses a mechanical device, which he calls a 'fortune wheel.' With the use of it he has so hypnotized his mind to mine that, with his mind, he reads mine, and with his follows me everywhere I go."

The writer then said he was followed to Durham, Wilmington, Newport News, Washington, New York, Boston, and other places, from which he can hear and communicate with him and others who are associated with him, just as well as if he were there (in his presence.)

"A woman"—he added—"an ordinary uneducated one has been so transformed by this Hitler with his 'wheel of fortune' that she, too, reads my mind even though I am a distance of about 350 miles from her."

"Others," my informant asserts, "are in this unusual crime, one of them young, the son of a very wealthy professional man.

"So far as I know I have never done any one in that city harm.

"It is said this business is carried on in a house, the owner of which is named. and the exact location given. These people ran cars in front of my door, from about 10 o'clock p.m. at night, until daylight the next morning. While this was going on Hitler was operating his wheel, and has fixed me so that I can hear them from there to Washington, D. C., and all other places I visit. But, they have also fixed themselves, they cannot leave there until judgment day, unless something is done for them.

"This has been and still is the most torturing experience that any human being has ever had, and I appealed to the mayor of the town and the board of county commissioners, the attorney general of the State, the Federal Bureau of Investigation, former Governor J. M. Brougton, Governor R. Gregg Cherry, United States Attorney General Tom Clark, D. Lamar Caudle, the Hon. J. Edgar Hoover, the late President Franklin D. Roosevelt, President Harry S. Truman, and, moreover, I have written to Senator Clyde R. Hoey, Senator Robert Taft, of Ohio, former Governor Darden of Virginia, and Governor Thomas E. Dewey, of New York."

The man is asking for an investigation.

"Since nothing like this has ever occurred I presume a majority of the men to whom I have appealed thought that I had an illusion but this thing really exists just as I have outlined it," he wrote. "Much damage has been done by it. If everyone connected with this unusual business were electrocuted or hanged that would not atone for the injury that has been done. If you find the woman and the young man referred to here you can then locate Hitler.

"This Hitler says he is an alien. I have never seen him but have seen the woman he uses for this trick.

"Now, Mr. Bryant, if you go to this town and investigate this matter you will expose the most unusual violation of law that has ever been committed on the American continent and so arouse the thoughtful and patriotic people of this country that they will then make a supreme effort to prevent a recurrence of anything like this in the United States."

In a letter I asked if the case had been looked into by any authority.

"So far as I know," said he in reply, "the matter has never been investigated although I have made an earnest and honest appeal to various high officials for an investigation. Senator Hoey wrote me a nice letter, but, seemingly, no one, except the people in the town involved, and who know about this situation, believe that anything like it can happen to a human being.

"So far as I am aware nothing like this has ever occurred before on the American continent, and I am unable to see how such a thing can be tolerated in any civilized community. That so-called 'fortune wheel' is doubtless one of the most dangerous instruments in the country. Its potential possibilities for much danger are very great. With an instrument like that, further perfected, almost any State or Federal secret might be revealed to avowed enemies.

"For a period of almost six years I have been tortured much by this thing. How I have managed to stand it this long Almighty God only knows. I would not have willingly had this wanton attack made on me for a million dollars in cash. Indirectly my family has been greatly damaged, and I have not had any permanent, gainful employment for about five years, nor have I had a night's real rest within that time.

"If it were possible to impress you with the importance of this story you would doubtless send someone to that city to investigate and make to you a confidential report.

"I am sure no other living human being has had an experience like mine.

"If someone would like to test this case I will go to Washington, D. C., or New York, and in the presence of witnesses open a sealed note—not open my mouth, and in less than one minute it will be repeated in the city of that 'wheel of fortune.' "

After receiving the second letter, a neighbor and I drove 60 or more miles to see the author of the letters, and the victim of the strange experience cited by him. We found him at his home, a rather pretentious one of his old family estate, and talked with him for nearly an hour. We learned that he was nearly 70 years old, an honor college graduate, and a man of good manners. The property on which he lives and calls his home contains 400 acres and six good mules are maintained the year 'round to till crops on it.

Having heard his story I asked him to write out what I could say about his troubles and in a few days I received a detailed account addressed to "Whom it may concern." His greatest desire is to have someone in State or Federal government authority to probe into the case and report on it. He would have the investigator start at the community in which he resided and worked for more than a decade, with especial attention to the drive made on him by the use of a chain of automobiles that paraded by his home, throwing their lights at him. His house, where he worked, had been owned by a well-known family before he purchased it. In his lengthy response to my request that he wrote out what I could say of his experiences, he said in part:

"By the constant use of that unusual and very powerful 'fortune wheel' Hitler has so hypnotized his mind and that of one or more of his associates to my mind that, with theirs, they follow me wherever I go in North Carolina, West Virginia, the District of Columbia, New York and Massachusetts, and from each and every place I can hear them.

"Hitler and his co-workers operate this instrument every minute of the day of 24 hours, some member of the group talking practically all of the time.

"Mine has been one of the most horrible trials any human ever had. I am at a loss to know why this secret and wanton attack should have been made upon me.

"All that I have asked thus far is for an investigation to ascertain the cause, and purpose of this drive. I would co-operate with State or Federal agents to get at the truth of this matter. After all of my appeals for help not one thing has been done about it. The people who have attached their minds to mine see whatever my eyes behold and hear whatever passes into my ears. The constant assault on me makes an impression on my mind. If this machine, which is now partially effective, were perfected no secret of any government would be safe. Even the atomic bomb would yield to it. It is dangerous to the extreme to permit it to exist, and operate. No person on earth, by looking at me, can tell any appreciable difference between me and any-one else, and yet, I can be eating or drinking in New York City or Boston, and at the same time communicate with those people back in North Carolina.

"I would be very grateful if scientists, psychologists, or other students of the mind would tell what they can to throw light on this mystery.

"One dreadful fact about all this is that anyone influenced by the Hitler party, aided by that wheel, can and does say whatever he or she likes and I am compelled to hear it. Sometimes the language is course and, at others, obscene.

"There is scarcely one in a thousand persons who believes that a thing like this can exist—not one in my own family thinks that it does as I have described it. But, it does. I am person-ally responsible for what I say, or may say hereafter, and have no fear of anyone who breathes the breath of life, and my chief aim is to warn the American people of an impending catastrophe whether they like it or not.

"If, and whenever this matter is investigated, I will be pleased to co-operate with authorized agents which may get information, the use of which may prevent a recurrence of anything as vile as this, anywhere in this land."

That statement was signed "A Citizen of the Commonwealth of North Carolina and of the United States of America."

My inquiry into this surprising and, to me, interesting case revealed that a very clever, carefully educated, and polite and courteous Negro wrote and mailed the letters to me. He is rather small, active and friendly. His manners are far gentler, and more refined than those of many white people I have met. He seemed very serious, but quite aggressive in his desire for an inquiry into his most unusual experience.

But, after pondering the communications, and interviewing the author all that I can say is: "The whole thing is above my head."

May 1, 1947
P. O. Box 154
Los Molinos California.

Dear Mr. Palmer and Mr. Shaver;

For some time I have been planning to write into fiction form some of the impressions I have experienced along with a word picture of the things that I too have seen. With a market in view I picked on Amazing Stories, only to find that my puny efforts would only be anti-climatic to the Shaver Mystery. I do feel, however, that the things that I have managed to dig up and the things that I have seen and learned thru projection and actual contact are worth adding to the collection.

Perhaps Mr. Shaver has the right idea in pronouncing his works as fantasy at the begin-ning to forstall any attempts to confine him to the bug house. I herewith do the same. I have no method on earth with which to prove the things that I have seen and heard thru projection, therefor they can be nothing but imagination. I can offer some visible evidence to some, such as the underground opening between Mt. Shasta and Mt. Lassen. You are aware, I take it, of the strange tales that have come from the Mt. Shasta district. I have personally witnessed some of these things. I have had the experience of a car motor failing to operate when trying to approach this area. I have seen the balls of light (I have a theory on these) Including those seen near San Jose, Cal. Also the strange sight of the supposedly large space ship that flirted around Modesto and told about in the Oakland Newspapers. One instance of strange phenomena that we witnessed here in this locality, which for your information is within 60 miles of Mt. Lassen and 150 of Mt. Shasta, was a play of light beams over the entire sky from horizon to horizon. The lights seemed to be more prominent around the two mountains. This could be the result of our seeing into the things what our minds would believe. In any event these beams, and they were beams and not northern lights, were white and golden in color and moved about with the same kind of motion as do searchlights playing about. Now I have played with high powered light beams and have seen many of them in operation and they all have a characteristic in common. They all spring from a ground source and it is easy to tell that they do, for the beam is traveling on a tangent to the onlooker in spite of the position of the viewer. I mean that the viewer cannot get into a position so the beam of a ground light would not appear to be on a tangent. These lights that we saw were not on a tangent to the surface of the earth but parallel to it and very high, (at least none of the beams ever spotted any surface object and this valley is rimmed with high mountains.) The horizon is not so far as might seem due to those same mountains. These lights were first noticed at about eleven in the evening and continued for nearly two hours then they began fading out until they were all gone. At first when they began to disappear it seemed that they began fading in luminosity but after they were nearly all gone it could be seen that it was a lessening of the light that gave this illusion. Really the lights were snapped off just the same as a ground searchlight. The whole country was lighted by the display, and the snow white tops of both Lassen and Shasta were plainly visible in the reflected light. There were only a few people saw this display as far as I could ever find out. When we began asking people if they had seen such a display we were given the fishy stare so that was where that phenomena ended.

I shall not bother you with details of more incidents but I feel that your attention should be called to the fact that there are many strange things happening in California that bear investigating and that seem to lie in the same category as those Mr. Shaver recounts.

There is another strange thing that has occurred in this same locality. There is a tribe of Indians back in the hills toward Mt. Lassen that have pestered stockmen for years. At one time they were very bold and many of them. They were mean and thought nothing of killing anything that came in their path. They took anything and everything that they could get possession of, and one time made off (so the story goes) with some white children, the people for miles around got together and herded as many as they could find into a bunch and killed them all. There were several that could not be caught off base, so to speak, for when they were pursued they were said to have vanished. Since that time of the massacre the Indians have not been so bold, but the cattle still vanish and there are still the same strange robbery stories popping up in the news. Every attempt to locate their place of abode and security has failed. They vanish into the canyons and shrubs. There are tales of their being able to get across ravines that the pursuers find impossible.

The payoff to this bunch of story material is that about four or five weeks ago a four motored plane on charter was passing over this territory. The plane was heard to pass over the Chico airport very low and was heard immediately after ten miles away still very low and headed for the mountains. The plane was contacted by radio and it made a large circle, following the identical path and on the second time no word was heard, just the roar of the motors as the airport attendants tried to get answers to their questions. That plane was traced by the noise and the radio to the hills in the proximity of the Indian stomping grounds and no sign nor piece of that plane has been located, and the search was made by helicopter and dozens of light planes and ground forces. It is even a mystery to the laymen as to the mission and intention of the men aboard the plane.

I said I was not going to bother with any more details, but that one was too talked about to miss. Like all others there is no end to the tales to be told.

To get back to the beginning. I was intending to try to incorporate into fiction my experiences of a nature similar to Mr. Shaver's tales. I must confess that I had no idea that Mr. Shaver or the Shaver mystery even existed until I read the edition of A S prior to the Shaver memorial. As I say my efforts would be puny I am afraid, so I shall content myself with relating some of them so that any information that may be of use can be filed.

In the first place would like to make one point. I do not believe it is the intention of Mr. Shaver to disclaim any possibility of the divinity of man. All our sources of information tell us that man has in his being a portion of creation itself, thereby making it entirely possible for him to have at his command a higher power that those of the five senses. It is even possible that the Elders of Shaver are the same as the Gods of Oahspe, and could very well be the Gods we in modern Christianity speak of. In fact if we look for the ultimate in all the propositions we find they are all compatible. Shaver leaving out any reference to the spiritual part of man's makeup tends to create an illusion that man is an animal from start to finish with no possible chance of any life in another plane. This is not in line with all early sources of information of an inspirational nature, or metaphysical teachings the world over. The law of coincidence alone would not permit all dogmas and theories on the things called man to have this one basic thing in common unless it were fact irrefutable.

We find, then, when we add this possibility to Shaver's facts the questions that have plagued man in BOTH planes or realms are somewhat clarified. ACCORDING TO THE STATE OF THE SPIRITUAL DEVELOPMENT OF THE INDIVIDUAL.

I make this approach because I have demonstrated that those methods and principles taught by the masters in the field of metaphysics will directly effect those rays of the ancient Mech. The strange feeling of being spotted by one of those beams is a very familiar sensation to myself and my family. And as always they are quickly dispersed or the operators quickly turn them away whenever one will project inward and toward the infinite source of energy and permit the body to be an agent or transmitter. In that fleeting second between one may receive some of the motivating impulses behind the beam itself. Investigation has proven to my own satisfaction that this ability is directly proportional to the real advancement of the individual.

When I speak of beams and rays in connection with the experiences that I have had I do not mean to imply that I have identified those things as having the same source as Shaver. Far from it. All I have ever been able to do is determine that there is an intelligence behind the feelings, and when they are black there is a human agency involved. I do not always sense this when the experience is on the white side. I am sure you will understand what I mean by black and white in these experiences so will offer no further explanation. Assuming that they do stem from Deros that still does not affect the point that I wish to establish first: that is that the degree of influence the white can have for an individual, or I might say the beneficial rays, is in direct proportion to the spiritual awareness possessed by that individual, and the amount of harm a stim ray can have is directly proportional to the amount of spiritual awareness NOT manifest by the individual, regardless if the individual is in possession of it or not. In other words one may have the awareness to some extent, but it is not an integral part of his being, and in that event whenever there is an occasion to use said knowledge it must be put into action with the will. This is the kind that is in the majority on earth today, and that accounts for the fact that incentives for motion have to be constantly placed into the social stream to prevent stagnation. Very few individuals have the ability to generate from within themselves; very few people make the truth a part of themselves so that action is instinctive, and therein lies the enigma of today. I have found that these two conditions are not normal and have nothing to do with normal projection. With normal projection or reception there is no feeling of strain or uncomfortable sensations.

Now to get back to the more direct connection to the Shaver mysteries. All of us have been dogged by this interest in the past of our race are well aware of the existence of the underground workings and places that exist in Mexico and Peru. In fact there was a pair of interesting notes to the same effect in the Memorial issue. In there it was stated that as yet no one has ever been able to find out what lies behind the barrier put up by the priests in the village of Xilitla. On the west side there is an opening that cannot be reached by any kind of surface vessel. I am sure Mr. Shaver will understand me when I say that I have been in and thru these workings many, many times, both on foot and by machine, but always by projection. You may decide on your own terms of expression for the experience. I call it projection merely because I have partial control of same. If it were otherwise I would be inclined to consider it accidental contact with thought record or some such condition. The fact of projection is about all I have had control of. The direction seems to be controlled from another source or condition, either time or space. In any event I have been in these caverns and can give a somewhat clear idea of their size shape and directional variations. The important features are what we are after now, however. One thing the entrance that has been plugged by the priests was put in that condition many years before there were any priests in that part of the country. In fact it was put out of commission from the INSIDE first. It is also blocked off very effectively about one quarter of the way thru the mountain and several levels lower. There is another opening on the east side some distance (this is something that I cannot give in any kind of veracity. I have tried for years to locate this other opening geographically but can only approximate it) and farther south than the one known about. After this tunnel has been traversed for nearly half the distance to the West side, and down I would say nearly a mile below the surface there is a branch line that runs (I think) south. It might go down first, but I have definitely been able to gather this from mental contact with some of the parties that I have seen there. I have never been able to penetrate beyond this point. I have, however, been taken for many a ride thru these workings and out through the West entrance. Here is a peculiar thing. The vehicles used here are the same ones that have been seen over San Francisco and northern Calif. at various times. I have seen these vessels myself with the physical eyes on two occasions. It is possible thru some kind of directional beam, to leave and enter this opening, which by the way is not very large, at considerable speed and with frightening accuracy. To get back to the branch going south. I am inclined to lean toward the idea that it is an elevator going down because in addition to the usual door-like blocking device there is also a gate that works automatically with whatever kind of device lies behind the door. From there your guess is as good as mine. Going back down the tunnel from this point to where the first tunnel comes into this main shaft. I am not clear on the distance from the entrance this point is, but the blocking that is here is really a job of masonry.

The one time that I ever inquired of my hosts of these tunnels about this sealed tunnel and what lies behind I was rewarded with the sensation of the most repulsive and evil state of existence that can be imagined. It seems that it is for that reason that it was closed off. Until the Shaver Memorial issue of A S I was in a quandry as to what shape these entities could be. As for the people I have encountered here. This can be brief for I have been permitted to contact only two, although I have seen many hundreds from varying distances. Sometimes I was denied even any recognition. On these instances there has been no evidence that there was any kind of equipment ever around, no people no nothing. Just bare tunnels. And if you think you cannot get tired walking even thru projection you should try these tunnels some time. When the hosts were there they always had lots of paraphernalia with them, and I was always there at their pleasure. Not much activity was ever in evidence, but always there were a few of the flying machines coming and going. Some would come from the southern branch and some would go to the same source. Others would come to the central assembly room and there they would stay as though resting before continuing on somewhere else. About these people. A few times I have tried to describe them. I have never made the attempt in the same place twice, I can tell you. I cannot even describe the sensation of physical excitement that accompanies the mere sight of one of them. As usual the most frequent host I have had has always been a young woman. I should say hostess. Many people express the thought that all S F stories are always telling of the terrific lure of these beings. They seem to think that it is all the work of a moral idiot. Well I can verify Shaver on that part of the contacts. Never in any physical existence can any one of the 20th century ever create such chaos and sublime ecstasy all in one instant. To have a being of this kind touch any part of the body is to have every cell in that body cry out for union and permanent association with every cell in the other being. The trouble arises in the fact that our filthy dogmas of modern education teach us to respond to anything that stimulates the cell structure in a purely animal manner, and if there are any laymen who think they have gone thru hell they should have to conquer this sensation and at the same time have the recipient of the lewd, silly thought impulses from the 20th century know every thought and feeling that is pounding and tearing through the body and soul. The male members of this society are not the degenerate kind that Shaver has pictured. They too create a stimulating sensation. Everything seems to be hastened to the perception. Ones awareness is very keen and I find that thinking in the abstract is quite simple, even into three and four dimensions removed. Enough for this part.

In Peru at the famous Lake Titacaca there are some Monoliths and an old ruins of what has been called a building. Either in or very close to these Monoliths is an entrance to a regular city under ground. At the ruins also there is an entrance, although I have never been able to find it. Maybe some of the boys down there on the job physically can. Every time I have landed there thru projection I have been too stupid to get in. I have always had to project into the place itself. This place is or was, it seems, a huge transportation depot or stopover place for travelers to and from the Pac. and the Atlantic, who were traveling by boat thru what is now South America. Only in two places in all my research have I ever found any reference to this fact, Churchward and an old MMS that I have been privileged to see that is in the hands of a very learned mystic and master. In each instance the drawings are the same, indicating that either one came from the other or they both came from the same source. I lean toward this latter for Churchward indicates the source of his information to be the same general locality as the other.

Only twice have I ever met anyone in this place and both times it was the same woman that was in the Mexico tunnels. Never seems to be any age attached to the time elapses that occur to me. Each time the meetings were as though we were on vacation. Nothing in particular to be done but wander around and look. I am a mechanical student and have made a living at the business of mechanics for years. At present I am teaching in a High School in that capacity. Naturally my interest has been toward the methods of operating the many machines that I have seen. And in Peru there are so many kinds of contraptions that it made my head swim to even try to fathom the fact of them let alone the principle. But I have gained this much. Those airships were motivated by a device that gathered energy direct from the atmosphere, without any motion. The energy was electrical. The device had plates very similar to our storage batterys. They were dry and seemed to be adjusted with micrometer screw arrangements. This gadget furnished the necessary power for the apparatus that propelled the vehicle. This part was beyond me, even though I saw the insides of the thing. It controlled the force of what we call gravity and itself be controlled by thought or mental emanations or waves by the operator. I do not think that we moderns could operate those ships if there were more than one passenger. I do not think that there could be a condition without a conflict of wills, and this machine is allergic to such states.

I have also seen a machine similar to the one Churchward describes as being like a triple turbine. These seem to work on somewhat the same principle as the collector mech. except it has the ability to rotate a shaft. I don't know what they were or are used for because I have never seen them connected to anything, and I have come on some of them humming along very serenely. The thing that prevents me from trying to duplicate the collector is the fact that I can not recognize any of the metals that were used. They are very definitely something the 20th century is not acquainted with.

So much for that. Mr. Shaver did not indicate clearly enough the intention and constancy of application of the Deros in their control of surface people. I cannot quite conceive that all the chaos and strife that we are experiencing can be the result of promiscuous tampering, but rather must be the result of very deliberate and malignant intention. Therefore there must be other sources of influence affecting the surface people.

As for the thought that there are not enough people who are interested to do any good, well I can agree with that. Even excepting the fact that there is a crackpot on every corner in Calif. There have been more plans for liberation of mankind spring up in Calif., than any other state in the union. I believe if enough publicity were given the cavern people the whole state of Calif. would be at the entrance. Not the least of these liberation movements here was called after the name of the book I have inclosed with this MMS. I picked up several copies in a second hand book store. I have had some contact with this outfit before they were driven underground (figure of speech) and I find the book interesting in several instances. However the thing that makes it interesting to the thing at hand is the fact that the leader or superintendent as he called himself, claimed that the spomsers and other divisions had at their command MACHINES THAT WOULD UPSET THE WORLD. These included a RAY that could set off any explosive made from cellulose within a radius of several hundred miles. It was also claimed for these Rays that they could transmit thought and even persuade people to do things that were contrary to the individuals wills. They also claimed to have (it was claimed by some of the inner members that they saw a demonstration of it) a gadget that could produce electrical energy without any external connections or help and no moving parts, and that such an instrument that could be held in the hands would furnish enough energy to light a small city. From the description that I have been able to get of the thing, it could very well be one of the same things I have seen so many times in my projections to the tunnels.

Take a look at this book and see if you get anything that would indicate any connection from your point of view, if not you may feel free to toss the thing into the waste basket. I have plenty more. I got two dozen for practically nothing.

As soon as the weather permits I am going to make a regular exploration of the caverns that are off towards Mt. Lassen. I will send you copies of what pictures I am able to get. Also I have taken a picture of one of these regions like Shasta, of a place that was supposed to have peculiar things going on. What the neg. registered was a conglomerate mass of blacks and whites with no gradation and if you look at it for a while you can see the figure of a face. And by stretching your imagination a little it will resemble pictures of what Jesus was supposed to look like. I made no attempt to answer this one. I know that the camera should have given a picture of a natural mountain side with trees and shrubs like any other side hill. I shall make a copy of this and send it at the same time. Sorry they are not prepared as of now but it will be at least two weeks before the snow is gone from the place where we must enter the caves.

Here's wishing all those who have peculiar things happen to them a bright new future in the very near future.

As I am a school teacher I would rather you would not get the urge to print this letter. If you are overcome just leave my name off the bottom. School Boards are very noted for their narrow mindedness and I feel that I can prepare more young people for the things that are coming to us all by remaining in the system. In Calif. we have a law forbidding even Jesus from preaching without first seeking permission from the powers that be.

There are so many factors envolving all of us in this coming era that any kind of statements pointing to the way are instantly construed as something for condemnation.

Let me know if there is any connection in all this that we know of in this part of the world.

Respectfully Yours,

## CREEPS

A thing that crawls like a great white spider through the endless forgotten labyrinths of wonder work, up and down the sheer walls of vast earth fault chasms reachable by no other agency than their prehensile pale hands and strange, long, creeping bodies. These are called "creeps" in the argot of the modern cavern dweller below the U.S.—and are despised parts of the weird landscape of the dark world. A something to be run over as one runs over a rabbit in the road—a something to laugh at as it yips in pain—a pain it has no words to express—

## BLOOD AND BRUTES

It wasn't nice. It wasn't fit to print. It wasn't anything arty, or beautiful, or delicate, the sky wasn't rosy with lace edged clouds.

But it was life, and he was going to write it that way. Blood beating against brute stupidity destroying man. The blood and brains and will of man against abysmal brutality, against the antitheses of art. Against the forces that have made life the unlivable mess of ugly dull painful nothing that it is for all of us, men without . . .

It was the Golden Apples of Idun, eaten by things vastly less than Jap beetles; tossed aside by things that ought to be man-like, weren't anything but insects eating the tree of man-life.

You know the legend of the Golden Apples? The Asgard heros ate them, stayed young and healthy. Loki stole them, hid away with them, and all Asgard withered and turned old.

Well, even today the Apples of Idun exist, a secret way of defeating the withering. It is hidden, nearly lost. But still—they exist!

He had said that before. It wasn't the way to say it. It should be said in pounding blows of fists on dying bleeding flesh, it should be said with poison in the reservoir making a whole town stupid for the rest of the peoples lives—after they drank the water. It should be said with disease germs dropped from planes, it should be said with sterilizing rays in virgin wombs emasculating the future children. Cutting off the future in the womb, rays on heads making of a race a stupid people without a future, only madness—*and the madness of stupidity can seem so sane!*

The Golden Apples of Idun is not a tale to drop lily-like from the window of an ivory tower. It is a tale to hammer out on an anvil of hot steel and bulging muscles and sweating limbs.

# READER'S SECTION
### Continued from Page 5

may lead.

Oh, yes, Mr. Shaver, here is another "sample of the green" to keep the club publication coming.

One other thought, Mr. Shaver, I doubt if you'll find the entrance you seek in any part of the eastern coast of either the U.S. or Canada, unless the ones now moving in here are able to defeat the entrenched forces already here as those in this section both in the States and Canada seem to be suffering very intensely from tamper. I say this from close observation, allowing for the differences previously noted. You might tell us how we common folk can help still further, for, brother, *we* REALLY need help in a common cause! We must either band together for good or go down separately into the caves as the "floor show"! "That ain't funny, McGee!" . . . J. F. Pearce, 48 Hubbard St., Malden 48, Mass.

*Dear J. F.:*

*Thanks. I am printing an old letter from MacDonald to show the thought and views behind his opinions of ourselves—or of myself—of spirits and occultism and etc. It is very enlightening and I trust he will not object.—Dick.*

Editor, Amazing Stories. Ziff-Davis Publishing Co.
185 North Wabash Ave., Chicago 3, Illinois    April 22, 1947
Dear Mr. Palmer:

The mountain has labored and brought forth a mouse! Your super-colossal de luxe special Shaver Issue, which caused you all the screaming meemies to get out was, to me, interesting in some ways but disappointing in others.

Your resume of the Mystery to date was concise and helpful; but it gave few facts not already known.

Mr. Shaver's own statements were very disappointing. from my point of view. To me, the whole crux of the so-called Shaver Mystery is whether or not Mr. Shaver actually HAS or HAS NOT been in the caves, in the physical body, as he claims; or whether he merely thinks or believes he has been there because of vivid "impressions" or visions, or other strange circumstances which he himself cannot explain.

If Mr. Shaver HAS been in any of these caves, he could surely tell us where they are located, near what cities, and how he got to the entrance, etc. So far, he has not done this anywhere. He did say something in one of his fiction yarns about being lured by a beautiful woman into a strange house and taken down flights of stairs. But he omitted to tell us in what city or town this house is located.

If there are as many caves as Mr. Shaver insists, why it is not possible for him to tell us (or some scientists) where they are and let some serious investigating be made. This is the sort of thing that can easily be checked up; but to date. Shaver has not helped us in this matter one iota. All he seems to do is scold us for wanting scientific proofs.

In my world travels I have been down in a number of unusual caves and mines. I have been down in a coal mine in Spitsbergen, near the North Pole; and I have in my possession some coal that I brought back from there as proof. I have been in several famous stelactite caverns, and have pieces of rock from them. I have salt from that salt mine under Detroit. Etc.

Now WHY cannot Mr. Shaver bring back some physical object from the caves he has visited? In his article, he scoffs at us for wanting him to do this very simple thing, and goes on to say that he could no more bring back an object from a cave than some ambassador could get proof in Russia that the people were contemplating a revolution! That is absurd reasoning, for it confuses the issue. A piece of stone or machinery or manuscript is not the same as intangible proof that somebody is going to start a revolution. The first is a physical object; the second is an invisible idea. The rest is material, the second is immaterial. Why is it so impossible for Mr. Shaver to pick up something from the floor of one of these caves, or ask one of his good friends there for a souvenir? I've even been in Russia, and have physical objects to prove I've been there in person. That's all we want, primarily, from Mr. Shaver—some physical proof which can be checked and verified. We don't want or expect him to bring us proof that the deros are *thinking* in a certain way.

To me, Mr. Palmer, this is the great weakness of the whole Shaver Mystery so far. Neither you nor Mr. Shaver has offered one iota of concrete, physical evidence that your author actually has been in any cave in his physical body. You speak about the necessity of investigating everything scientifically; yet in this most vital matter, you and Shaver shy away from it, and give a lot of "deductions" and talk; but nothing that impartial scientists can examine in a laboratory and check upon what it is, etc. Until you and Shaver do this, I for one will be skeptical that he has ever been in the caves *in person.* And I don't think I am being unreasonable in not accepting mere sophistry.

On the other hand, it is entirely possible that Mr. Shaver has had some dreams or visions and honestly THINKS he has been down under the ground. This is a very different matter. There are today thousands of people, both professional and nonprofessional mediums, who are clairvoyant and clairaudient, and who have many vivid experiences which seem very real to them. In trance, they actually feel themselves in strange places, talking to strange people (those of the Other Spheres), and have experiences which they remember so vividly that it is hard for them to determine whether or not they were psychic adventures or physical adventures. Every student of Spiritualism and the occult sciences knows all about such examples of psychism, and accepts them for what they are. Many people who are extremely clairvoyant and clairaudient can read the Akashic Records, that is, see and the hear the events of the past which are recorded on the fine substance surrounding the earth known as the *akasa*. By reading the Akashic Records many mystics and mediums have gone back thousands and millions of years in time and "seen and heard" things happening at the time they actually did. And the impressions of these events seen clairvoyantly are so strong that the medium is able to report them exactly as if he or she had really been there in person.

There are more people who are powerful mediums of this sort than you may realize. I myself know a woman in New York City who can read the Akashic Records and describe to you what is taking place eons of time ago. She can contact your own psychic aura and tune in on your past incarnations and describe the high spots of several of your former lives. And while she is thus psychically tuned to the vibrations of the *akasa,* she "sees" and "hears and even feels and smells everything going on in the past! One time she was describing to my wife a scene in a very small, fiery planet millions of years ago; and as she talked she began to perspire all over her body (tho it was the middle of Winter in New York City and cold in her apartment) and cried out in anguish that she was being burned alive. It was a graphic scene for her and for us; and even when she had come out of her semi-trance condition, she was still sweating and afraid of the flames she had "been in."

People like myself who have spent half their lives studying psychic phenomena (scientifically) understand such things perfectly, and know all about them. There is a vast literature on the subject, too, which you and Shaver would do well to consult, seriously; for it might explain a great many things that you don't seem to grasp even yet.

I don't like to make a positive statement, because I feel that I do not know all the facts; but as a tentative theory, I would certainly say that Mr. Shaver has not been in any cave in his physical body; but that he is a medium, with a certain degree of clairvoyance and clairaudience already developed, and consequently he has "seen" and "heard" a great many curious things and has some experiences in the Lower Astral Realms (the bad ones, like Hell of the Christians) which have been so vivid to him that, not understanding psychism, he honestly believes that he has been to these places himself. But because it is all so strange and frightening to him, he is not able to give any concrete evidence of having been there in person; and so falls back upon deductions and inferences, and scolds the rest of us for not believing him!

There is hardly a thing that you or Mr. Shaver has said so far which cannot be explained on a psychic basis; and this explanation, instead of being far-fetched, is entirely in accord with the most ancient teachings of the mystic sciences. Thus, if this theory is correct, there is no "mystery" here at all!

In your editorial, you said Mr. Shaver was a materialist, who did not believe in Life After Death, or the soul, or anything of the sort. That being the case, there is NO WONDER that he is scared to death and is having such horrible "experiences." When a person who does not understand, or accept, Life After Death and the fact of spirit communication, becomes clairvoyant and clairaudient, he is open to the lowest class of spirit people—the former criminals, drunkards, jokers, and evil doers—who take possession of his psychic faculties and talk to him without restraint. They describe the spheres in which they themselves are now dwelling; and because they are evil people, not yet reformed and promoted to the high spirit realms, they know only the frightful Lower Astral Realms, which are pretty terrible. Many, many mediums have given accounts of these Lower Spheres, and they tally pretty well with Shaver's description of the caves and the deros, etc. If Mr. Shaver were a spiritual man, or a sincere seeker after spiritual enlightenment, the entities that he would contact would be finer people, and the "places" which he would "visit" would be more beautiful than his caves. The more spiritually developed the medium, the finer the guides; and the more the medium understands of the Life After Death, the more wonderful are the spheres he is permitted to see and "visit" psychically. Mr. Shaver is thus meeting and seeing exactly the sort of people and places he is entitled to because of his stage of spiritual comprehension. This is a LAW, which we all understand.

One thing I was interested in in your editorial, my friend. That was that you made a grudging admission that perhaps there might be something true in some of the things the Spiritualists had been telling you! That's fine. You claim to have made considerable research into Spiritualism. I hope you have; but to do it correctly, you would have to devote many years to it. You seem to think that "Spiritualism is a proof" of the Shaver mystery. No, it's just the other way around! But the fact that you have even come this far, is good.

(Readers—note above—Shaver).

So much for this. I hope you will devote more time to a real study of the occult sciences—NOT Oahspe. You will live to regret your foolish enthusiasm for that work. At first, to a person who has never investigated any occult matter serious, Oahspe seems like a miracle. But as a matter of fact, it is not accepted by any advanced student of the mystic sciences or Spiritualism as being a 100% genuine revelation. Some of it is O.K.; but most of it is hooey. I could mention two dozen real standard occult books that would make your hair curl, and which are accepted as authentic by the greatest scholars in the country. But if you persist in placing your faith in Oahspe, serious scholars will laugh at you, and you will get nowhere with any of this Shaver Mystery.

Just a few more thoughts in closing: Why in God's name drag in the Devil's Tower? I've seen it, close too, and I don't believe it's a petrified tree. But even if it were; what would that prove? Merely that at one time in the remote past there had been one extra large tree! How does that prove the existence of caves under the ground, filled with deros and ray machines? And how does all this prove that Mr. Shaver has had the experiences he says he has???

Your Shaver Language is more interesting from the occult point of view. This may well be a genuine revelation of some sort. Occasionally the spirit guides and teachers permit some authentic bit of information to come thru an ignorant, materialistic medium; for they figure, do the spirit teachers, that coming thru such a channel the information will reach certain individuals who would not see it if it were given only in seances, or before psychic research groups, or home circles. So, once in a while, we find somebody getting some authentic revelation from the spirit world, and giving this information to mankind. I don't know, of course, whether this Mantong is or is not the basic language of humanity. It may be. We'll have to investigate THIS further. But to me, a serious student of the Ancient Wisdom, this is one of the most interesting things you have published.

I trust in the future Mr. Shaver will tell us more definitely what it is all about; and I trust that you, friend, will stop running around in circles and turn to the only people who can really help you: the students of the occult sciences.

I'll reserve judgment and comment till further information is forthcoming from you. Good luck, and don't be frightened of the deros. They are merely evil, degenerate spirit entities who cannot harm you if you seek the proper, higher spirit protection, or have faith in some religion. Yours truly, Howard B. MacDonald.

*Letter, which to me, proves the nature of spiritualist beliefs to be blinding to those who seek actual material truth and defense against those whom Mr. MacDonald dismisses as "merely" spirit entities who cannot harm you. I know they can and do harm us all.—Richard S. Shaver.*

*Note—to occultists—I want it made clear I do not disbelieve in the possibility of spirits existing, or in any way set the magazine against spiritualism itself, but only against those who to my mind misuse great teachings to further their own individual viewpoints. I do not consider myself a student of occultism, but many occultists insist I am mediumistic and do not realize the fact. If the magazine proves interesting to occultists, that is fine and is my purpose. But my own viewpoints are entirely material and I have no personal experience with any phenomena which to me prove the existence of souls or living spirits on earth. All the occultists I have met have done so in a neutral spirit of inquiry and curiosity, and I wish in no way to interrupt this exchange of viewpoints and information between studious and sincere readers—whatever their personal opinions or beliefs. Believe me—there can be spirits—and nothing of what we are attempting will harm anyone who believes in the occult viewpoint. But I think such writing as MacDonalds is harmful in obscuring the actual danger of the underworld behind a facade of false wool about "spheres of lower entity" and thereby keep from general knowledge the actual work of enemies of our life. Please study his letter for this bad influence so you can recognize and not contribute to it.*

An important letter for the technically trained reader—and others!—Editor.

Dear Mr. Shaver:

Re the "Round Table Discussion" in the lastest issue of the club magazine:

Hope some of the electronic technicons among the members (if any) try out the Prof's idea for a televisor ray. I'm particularly interested in this for a reason I didn't mention in the original letter. It seemed too damned silly at that time. Since then, I've been wondering. I'm not a expert typist, but can usually copy fairly accurate. In this case, however, I had to copy that particular page six times before I got it right. The last time was letter-by-letter, and word-by-word. The error each time was in the professor's statement about the rays, and usually wasn't apparent at first glance. However, they changed the entire sense of what he said. It almost seemed as if someone didn't want this information made public—which makes me think that it *might* be important. If this was actually a case of tamper, it doesn't seem likely that it was a goon or rod, as they would probably have taken more drastic action. Maybe someone "just playing"?

There's another thing that might be worth some technical checking, if possible. I mentioned it once in a letter to Geier, but didn't go into detail. To supply the missing details: I was reading the article "20 Million Maniacs", in the first issue of "Fate". When I read about the woman who claimed that she, and several thousand others, had been secretly sensitized with selenium so that they could hear secret "radio broadcasts" urging them to various evil deeds, I got a peculiar and very strong impression. Let's call it a "hunch", for want of a better name, but I don't think it came out of my own brain. Here it is:

Her story is true. It's a new mass-production technique to replace older and slower methods of influencing people. A receiver can be built, using a selenium photo-electric cell and a radio receiver, which will enable anyone to hear the "broadcasts", thus proving her statement. The cell should have a filter on it, either infra-red or ultra-violet—not sure which. The beam isn't either of these, but the filter will cut out the ordinary light, which might cause trouble unless the outfit was used in total darkness. There was some brief thoughts about poloroid filters, but this seemed to finally lose out.

. . . something about V.V.H.F. V.V.H.F. won't pick it up, but the tuning is similar. Outfit connects grid to filament potentiometer blade. Some confusion as to whether it is hooked to a radio or audio stage. (There seemed to be two different lines of thought, which did not always agree with each other.) It works as a convertor—by-pass the regular set tuning. If I knew more about radio circuits, I might have gotten a clearer idea, but I've put it down just as it came into my head. If there are any radio "hams" in the club, maybe they can unscramble it. Or maybe I'm just plain nuts?

More of the same "hunch": Might not have much luck in this area. Very infrequent here?? Better luck in Chicago, New York or Washington. They're all bad?? Chi is very Bad?? Stay away from Mass., Penna., and Cal., with it. You sure *would* go nuts if you listened to *that???* It doesn't make sense to me, but maybe it will to you. Or maybe I'm merely getting nuttier as I go along.

I can understand your feelings toward those who know but won't talk, such as the professors, etc., but can see their point of view too. The Profs, for instance, have plenty of trouble buying groceries for their families as it is, on their pay. Boards of Regents aren't noted for being broad minded. "After all, you know, we gotta be careful what sort of ideas are being put into the heads of our children. Can't have any damned Bolsheviks, or anyone else with screwy ideas teaching them." It's not necessary to prove that a teacher is unorthodox. They only have to be suspected of it. "Can't be too careful, you know." We all realize that everyone ought to stand up for what they know is right regardless of anything, and that it's the best for themselves in the long run. But they have to eat in the short run. Today's problems are here to be solved right now. "Maybe tomorrow's problems won't ever arrive. Or maybe someone else will solve them, and we won't have to bother. So let's be cautious." . . . and so on. Some few may be willing to talk about it in private, as the ones in the discussion group, but you probably won't get much public support from them. You might get some from the students.

As for the scientists—there are scientists and scientists. Few of our "leading scientists and engineers"—the ones you read about in the papers—will give you any support. Few of them actually invent or develop anything. They're merely the organizers and executives. The actual work is done by a bunch of nameless Joes you never hear about. The scientific brass merely takes the bows, poses for the photographers, and issues the public statements. Half the time they don't even know what they've really invented or developed. Their "explanations" of how it works and what it will do are very amusing to those who really know. As for the technical Joes who do the actual work, I think you might get a lot of support from them. There are a few who are so fresh out of college that they haven't yet found out what the score is, and a few others brown-nosing to be a "leading scientist or engineer" themselves, but the others might help all they dared. That's the main trouble—fear for their job.

Mosts of these technical Joes have degrees, but don't let that worry you. They have to have them to get their job. I have a few letters that I can toss after my name whenever I want to tell anyone of equal or lesser rank that their ideas are wormy—but that's the only practical use I've found for it yet. As for their technical "education", most of them who have been in the racket for any length of time have thrown away about 50% of what they've learned (as I have) and are suspicious of the other 50%. The ordinary Joe may suspect that all the "facts" he's fed aren't strictly on the up and up—but the technical Joe knows damned well they aren't.

He also knows that, in many cases, the "brass" hampers progress, rather than making it. When research has produced *an* answer to the problem, it stops. It's probably not the best answer. First guesses seldom are. But why waste any more time hunting for something when you have already found it? The project is completed. And anyhow, we've got to get going and incorporate it into out Whatsits before Whosis & Co., get on the market with theirs. Possibly the thing has possibilities more important than the original aim, but our "leading scientist or engineer" can't see it. He's done what the directors want done, so that's that.

Take Radar, for instance (go ahead, *take* it, *I* don't want it!) For its much publicized purpose, it's a lemon. But it does happen to be the crude beginnings of some of the cavern mech, and the principle could be developed. Not by our scientific brass, perhaps, but some of the Joes who really developed it might do it. I only know what I've heard. Maybe it's only a rumor.

If you're interested in rumors, I also heard that the principles of gravity nullification, or whatever you want to call it, are used by every radio tube ever made. Someone seemed to be very amused that we had had the secret all this time, but were too dumb to recognize it. That's all I heard. "If we weren't bright enough to see it, to Hell with it." Maybe some of the bright boys in the club can take it from there. I can't. My line is mechanical engineering. I don't con electronics well enough to do it. All I can do is pass along anything that pops into my head that looks like a hint. If anyone can make anything of it—O.K.

I realize that your correspondence is heavy, and don't want to be responsible for hampering any club work (which is more important than answering letters) so do not request or expect a reply to this. If there's anything in it of value, the club is welcome to it. If not, file it in the nearest wastebasket. If I hear anything else that seems to be of any importance, I'll send it along —Yours very truly, J. A. McKee.

Dear Mr. Shaver:

Enclosed find one dollar for next two issues. I trust that ere long there will be more like you to show the courage to stand forth and show the Truth of things that have long befuddled peoples minds. I wish you every source of success in your venture and you can be sure I will spread your words as far as I am able.—Sincerely, Forest R. Harvey, 5819 Seventh Ave., N.W., Seattle, Wash.

*Dear Mr. Harvey:*

*Thanks a million for your encouraging words. I think that there will be more soon, and that is the core of my effort—and you are part of the product—a man who sees that the effort can be made and is not futile. I know there are many like you spreading the truth as well as ferreting out more truth for we who are the disinherited of earths real treasures from the past. I know that something real and worthwhile will come from the efforts of the many like yourself —soon or late. If we all work for that, even when we can't fully see how it will profit us— men cannot be losers because of our efforts.—Sincerely your friend, Richard S. Shaver.*

Dear Sirs:

If you file your correspondence, you will find a letter there from this writer which was written in the early part of this year, advising you of reading my first Amazing Stories magazine and of my instant interest in the magazine, especially the articles concerning Mr. Shaver and the caves. I haven't missed a copy of A. S. since then and interest in the mystery of the caves has grown until you may class me as an unofficial member of the CHMBS. In fact, the purpose of this letter is to inform you of a recent expedition to one of the caves for an investigation.

For you and those interested in the "air shaft" near Burley, Idaho, reported by Mr. George Haycock, whose letter was published in the October issue of A. S., this is to verify the truth of this cave.

M/Sgt. Roy W. Brentlinger (a Shaver fan), stationed at Hill Field, Utah, and myself made a trip to Burley over the week-end of the 17th of August to ascertain the authenticity of both Mr. Haycock and the cave. We had no trouble locating this gentleman and after explaining the purpose of our mission, he quite readily agreed to show us to the cave and to guide us through, providing it was still possible to enter. The entrance had been blasted since he was last in the cave, he explained.

We drove about six miles west of town, then turned off the highway onto a little road leading through the desert sage-brush. Oddly enough, this road was well worn and seemed to be much used, although there is no apparent reason for so much traffic. We failed to see any other cars either on the way in or out.

Even though he had been to the cave many times and to the entrance as recent as three days prior to this trip, Mr. Haycock, strangely, had difficulty in locating the spot and we stopped twice to look before we finally found it about a mile from the highway.

The entrance was located in the center of a shallow circular depression. The surrounding terrain was nothing but sand and sagebrush but jammed in and around the opening were several large boulders. We found there was still a small hole running down through the boulders and Mr. Haycock thought it still possible for us to make entrance. With some violent maneuvering we did manage to squeeze through and we followed Mr. Haycock to the floor of the cavern. Then, crawling, kneeling and sometimes walking, we were led back through the cave for approximately one-quarter of a mile.

The cavern is cut through what appears to be lava rock. Walls and ceiling are badly fallen-in in many places but there is enough intact yet to give the general impression that the cave was at one time square. In certain spots the walls and ceiling are perfectly flat. Then, too, we noticed one small chamber to one side of the main passage that is square-cut except for one end which is cupped-out.

There are numerous small passages leading off to the side of the main path, which Mr. Haycock said led to dead-ends; in the ones he has explored.

After seeing enough to convince us of the truth of Mr. Haycock's story, it was decided to turn back and not to continue inward to the impassable obstruction, Mr. Haycock mentioned in his letter. To have gone that far, more equipment would have been required. We had nothing but two flashlights, both being used continuously. Where we turned back is approximately half-way to the obstruction.

We failed to hear or feel the icy wind that is said to blow from the shaft most of the time.

However, Mr. Haycock explained that it did become quiet occasionally, as we found it that day.

At present another trip is planned to the cave. This time there will be seven or eight of us and we plan to take the proper equipment and enough provisions to do some serious work at clearing away the obstruction. It is desired by all to learn what, if anything, might lie further on beyond this obstruction. But, if there is nothing but more cave, it will at least be an interesting adventure that will be enjoyed and remembered by all!

Now for information on two other caves this writer knows of which might merit investigation: The first is in the Smoky Mountains of N. C. in the Nantahalie (?) Gorge. It is called "The Blowing Springs" and is easily reached from the highway. The cave has an icy blast of air and a cold stream flowing from it continuously, from which it got its name. It is not known by the writer whether anyone has ever entered this cave or if this be possible, but there are many that have been to the entrance to look in.

The second is called "The Devil's Well" and is located in the "Hole-In-Ground" near Pine City, Washington. The cave is very round and approximately five feet in diameter. People are known to be afraid to enter this cave due to the rumor that it is a rattlesnake den. It would be interesting to learn if there is any truth to the rattlesnakes and why it was named "THE DEVIL'S WELL", and by whom!—Sincerely yours, Frank W. Haigler, Box 18, Apt. F-22, Sahara Village, Utah.

Dear Mr. Shaver:

Have read, I believe—just about all the stories and articles written by you and about you in Ziff-Davis magazines. Also Sh. M. Magazine (even FATE).

Confess I've retained precious little, because to me taken as a whole it appears quite confusing; for instance, why can't you point out the same entrance to the caves "Nydia" led you through and especially go there with others?

Are you still—now—in "touch" with any of the Teros?

If they want to help the surface people, the deserving ones at least, why their insistence on concealment?

Mr. Shaver, just actually what are you "preaching" about? Specifically, why don't you advise in precise words what should be done? You keep "harping"—excuse the expression—(excused, RS) about time running out, but what must be accomplished to offset this???—inevitable doom???

In your answer to Mr. MacDonald (last issue SMM) your ending line signifies "more to come".

Won't you write, (and not in stories) what else in the future is to "to come"?

Will close for now and may I add Sincerely, but not convinced, yet.—V. Wood, 5513 Stone Ave., Cleveland 2, Ohio.

*Dear Mrs. Wood:*

*A lot of people ask me why don't I show the entrance to the underworld. I can only say—you can't get in without inside help—and the people who were there then are no longer there. They are dead, so far as I know.*

*Yes, I'm in touch. They do not insist on concealment—it is a secret keeps itself through general inability to accept the unusual or astonishing as actual.*

*Specifically, I'm preaching that the culture and science and wisdom of a very superior race is being lost by the men of earth to spoilers from space who for the most part have little appreciation for the value of what they destroy. We could get some of that wisdom, but we do not try, through ignorance, fear and general backwardness.*

*What should be done? Nationwide effort of a conscious, directed kind toward obtaining any part of that treasure below the rocks would result in a vast acquisition of new material for the growth of our national culture, scientifically and aesthetically. This effort is not made through a stupid incredulity and fear on the part of those people who should know far better.*

*"Time running out"—every day more of that wonder mech and forgotten recording of a superior races wisdom is carted off to space—or to storerooms under earth—more and more of the still un-despoiled living place of a vastly superior race is vandalized and ignorantly mired—lost to study of any kind.*

*There is no inevitable doom except the continuance of a bond of ignorance that ties us to a dying world.*

*Future to come, you ask? Either we learn the Wisdom of the Elder Race, or we perish in wars of our own making, or we stumble on and on in repetitive advance and loss—The Elder Race understood why people make war—and what to do to stop it. Their records contain exactly that knowledge we need most—how to stop and contain evil—how to grow and heal and make able minds to lead. . . .*

*All this you cannot accept because you have not seen—but I try to show you God-work with a mortal hand. Hard to do. . . . Shaver.*

Dear Mr. Shaver:

I don't want you to get the impression that only "older people" read your stories! When "I Remember Lemuria" was first published I was only 13 yrs. old, and from that time on I haven't missed a story.

But the main reason for this letter is to get rid of a few questions that have disturbed me long enough.

1. You say that you have teros who guard you from the rays of the deros. Now if that is true they live in the caverns under the area in which you live, since their protective rays can only travel a distance of about 50 miles. I was wondering why they couldn't teleport you into the caves any time they wished? Or you wished?

2. If the earth came from outer space like it says in Mandark, the core of this planet would be cold. Now where do volcanoes come from?

3. I know a good proof for the Shaver Mystery! Why can't you have one of the tero talk to someone over a telaug beam? I would love to be that person! (They may talk to you. —RS).

Please print this in the Club Mag, because I would like very much to know the answers to my questions.—A faithful follower, Wayne Lee, 213 Blake St., Indianapolis, Ind.

*Dear Wayne:*

*Talking to you is something I planned for, five years ago. To someday talk to a young mind that grew up through the formative period with the thoughts and knowledge that took me a short lifetime to acquire. Someone who knew from early youth that the world was not their oyster—but something they shared with very greedy neighbours. Someone who knew the Elder race existed and that Mantong was not a fiction—knew it ever since they began to think seriously. You should be very different in your thinking from the average man.*

*Have you learned to think with Mantong? Will you give it a little time every day until you can defend it against the modern pedant? Its the most needed and important job you could do for future man!*

*Q 1. About the teleport, I do not know for sure that it exists. It is much rumoured and talked about—so I included it in my stories. But I do not know it exists.*

*Q 2. I do not know the earth came from cold space—from outer space. I deduced that it did—because it seemed to me that the first great caves must have been bored in earth by a people seeking refuge from cold. But it could have been true that were bored to form a refuge from heat waves to come from the sun. It was a heat wave from our sun that killed off earth's Elder race.*

*Q 3. The tero have talked to lots of people over ray—as you can see by their letters. I have one here now from J. F. Pearce, 48 Hubbard St., Malden, Mass., write to him.—Dick.*

Dear Mr. Shaver:

Enclosed one dollar for *next* 2 issues of club magazine. Just finished your last one containing more "Mandark", and the beautiful girl with small skulls floating around her. Is she supposed to be Lila? I suppose it is just a symbolic picture to represent a sadistic beauty who scatters death; her dupes being the 44 skulls. Well, it is a great picture, but I don't quite understand the big beauty on front cover. However, you know how to put over the weird and keep us all guessing. After all, Life seems to be arranged for us in such a way that no matter what we learn we are still mystified; if it were not so we would have no need of evolution. Put that in your pipe and smoke it. I think it would be a grand past-time to carefully go over *your* stories and life history and work out a psychological sketch of *you;* you have such a colossal brain, but I'm afraid you are too pessimistic. You and the many writers who tell us that the next few years will see our finish are not helping people to settle anything. Thousands upon thousands of humans are ready to spend their remaining days in an orgy of debauch because they believe there is no use trying to improve; their philosophy is—like that of the scared child who says "the bogey man is coming." The Reds, the Shaverites, the Bomb experts, the Cancer goblin and political tricksters have made the American people crazy. Another class are trying to wipe out Christianity; and that, with its many good influences is about all we have left to comfort people and keep them decent.

In your tales you attempt to explain Spiritualism by your "mech" and fail to tell the public the good side of the oldest religion of the world. You also doubt there being a hereafter for us after the body is destroyed. Do you know we all are spirits and that our bodies are only vehicles to get experience in a physical world? Then, in another yarn we find you reversing your position and talking like an occultist but we always hang over the abyss by a hair, and you see no continuity for a human soul. As a Bible student you are a wonder but make the same mistakes of those you criticize: you quote the book to uphold your doctrine only. Nostradamus and hundreds of other prophets who forsaw the future by Bible study, Nature study, Astrology and other means are ignored. Anybody who studies Astrology enough to interpret his personal horoscope from a natal chart can soon realize that "mech" underground has nothing to do with his bad aspects. And how come you know nothing about people who follow New Thot, Unity, Christian Science and the other Faiths and make a success of their lives in spite of all the underground "mech"? I would like to see more tolerance shown by everybody and I think a lot of our fears can be licked if we just make up our minds to boss ourselves In fact I have done just that now in my old age (70). The way I feel about Life is, that the

Big Power that made the Cosmos or Kosmos is watching and sustaining it and often does send some special help to worthy people in trouble individually and collectively. I find so many people so ready to argue instead of building character and improving themselves. Your theory of radium causing death may be true, but the Power that stands back of all matter and other forces is not going to let a few million dero or a dinky Sun spoil the Kosmos. Now, as to the Gods, you credit no superior power beyond them and you say they made us, *and there you stop.* Who or what made the Gods or the Universe!

My uncle used to say: "Everything in life was a wheel within a wheel, but he knew as well as you and I that somebody made the wheels. Well, I must close this ramble and feed the inner man (another mystery). Some of the Catholic Church fathers have lived on bread and water for years. I'm as willing to believe *that* as I am that Shaver was delivered from prison by a spirit like Paul of old. Why not write that story for us Mr. Shaver? Feature it, give us all the details and facts, and prove it by news clippings and other testimony. Will be glad to get remainder of "Mandark" and your so-called proofs of the Underworld. Maybe lots of Planets have underworlds and Gods. Well, your story is not new. C. W. Leadbeater printed a book many years ago thru the Theosophical Society at Benares India about a cave in Cashmere that held a duplicate of every machine ever made by man. You ought to read Leadbeater's books too.

Yours for a better world,
V. G. Van Dalinda.

*V. G. Van Dalinda*
*1180 Goffle Road,*
*RFD 1 Wyckoff, N. J.*
Dear Mr. Dalinda:

*You are right there are many things I don't know. I do not have any colossal brain, and I do put a lot of things in my pipe to smoke and remain mystified after smoking—just as you.*

*The many writers who tell us that the next few years will see our end have a lot of things to back them up—man has always had a war in the making—and the next war, with atom bombs, is very apt to see the end of all of us is quite true.*

*But according to many spiritualist writers, and according to Oahspe as well as the bible— God himself cleans off the earth every so often to set it straight again. You can find that in your bible easily enough. So if we have souls, I don't see what there is to worry about in the impending doom.*

*My own teaching, that wars and evil are the result of "de", disintegrant energy distorting thought into destructive patterns, also is pessimistic as you say—but only so long as men remain ignorant of the cause of war and do nothing to counteract the constant influx of destructive impulse in general thought. If you had read all my stories you would have seen that carefully worked—not as a pessimism, but as a guide post to the only possible path to avoid future wars. This teaching is a deep basic need in man's life—and so far I am the only writer I have ever heard of espousing this truth. I would like to read Leadbeater but I have never run across his writings—if you could loan me? I would return, and give other books to read while I retained your Leadbeaters.*

*I don't know whether you are intimating I am one of those who "try to wipe out Christianity" but if so, you are wrong. I think Christ saw a great truth and expressed it in his own words. It is much the same truth I express—he called it "love" and I call it "integrative patterned thought". It is much the same, and Christ was probably the more understandable in his time.*

*My explanation of the cause of evil is not my own—but is a v basic Elder race teaching. It is even more important than Christ's teaching of "love" and etc. So far as I know I am the only writer trying to carry on and perpetuate these vital basic truths—which are the same truths, though vastly differently interpreted—as Christ and the Church teach. I think my teaching is broader and more important and better founded in logic. So do those who understand me. But they are distinctly NOT opposed.*

*I do not say that spiritualists are wrong. I see little evidence on earth of soul continuity of the kind they teach. But I do see a vast creative life force and its continuity—but I see it as a misunderstood and misinterpreted force. I try to present my own view of the life force for a more constructive attitude toward life and its propagation and enrichment. I do not in any way want to discourage other views of the life force and its nature. Neither do I believe in perpetuating fallacies, because they are pleasant and comforting fallacies.*

*One of these fallacies is the conviction that because we have an immortal life after death we do not have to fight age and death as evils. See what I mean? Wouldn't you prefer a doctor who knew what to do to defeat death from age to one who did not—because that Doctor thought it was better for you to die and go to heaven than to continue on earth?*

*If there is something in us that lives after our body dies and is embalmed—fine. But to accept that as a truth and abandon all ideas of trying to lengthen life is wrong. I sincerely believe that immortals do not die because they do not die—not because they have died many times.*

*It is quite possible that there are ethereal planes of life too tenuous for mortal eyes to detect—and that we graduate into them after death. But until we KNOW it from observable and pragmatic tests and proofs—it is better that we try harder to make something of this life we are sure exists.*

*Astrologers may be right in their ideas of star influence upon our character and fate—but I personally have no good reason to think so. I know nothing whatever about is true.*

*You say that followers of New Thought, Unity, Christian Science, etc., make successes of their lives—and I know nothing of it. That is true, I don't.*

*Truth is, I do not think any mortal man is making much of a success of life—because each of them suffers the same mortal ills, hodcarrier or millionaire—and dies about the same time. One is in reality little luckier than the other, or more of a success, from my point of view—a view considering actual life value. The hodcarrier is healthier than the millionaire because he keeps his body active and able—but he has to use his health in unpleasant labor—both are losers. That is the way I see it, they are all vastly mistaken in their values, and would all do very differently if they thought more clearly.*

*I know people get special help from unseen sources. I too see Life as a big creative force behind all things. I too believe in vast and superior intelligences of omniscient and inscrutable nature. But I do not agree with those who lean upon such ideas and expect them to order their world for them. They just don't work that way.*

*I think there are superior powers to the Gods about whom I write. But I can see no way our mortal minds can grasp or comprehend what they are about, or their purposes. And I do not accept the belief that such minds find us important, or care what becomes of us.*

*My story is coming out in a book called the Elder World soon, which will contain everything I can put in as well as my autobiography. It will have all the details and facts I can lay hands on.*

*Hoping we understand each other better now, and knowing we each have something to tell the other, hoping I have understood you and that you will see what I mean, too—I remain your friend. Richard S. Shaver.*

Dear Sir:
Enclosed are the pictures taken in the caves outside of Mexico City.

An Eastman camera was used and time exposure given. The first shot taken in the cave came out good, after that all the photos—shots of the rest of the cave had these light scrolls.

In your opinion what could they be and what could cause them to register on a film—in this manner?

Thanking you in advance for any information, I remain very truly yours—C. H. Robinson, 13121 Osborne St., Pacoima, Calif.

*Dear Mr. Robinson:*
*Photos look as if a number of small watch rays had approached you, taken a look—listened for a moment to your thought, found you harmless—and went away again. What else could cause these scrolls of light—? You took them, you know they were not faked.—Sincerely, Richard S. Shaver.*

Dear R. S.—
Ask and ye shall receive, seek and ye shall find, knock and you will have lots of company —so—as if you didn't have enough troubles, here's me again. Anyhow, my friend, I appreciate your taking the trouble to answer my recent outburst, in spite of your vast correspondence— and so, since you faintly suggested that I write again, you may blame this on yourself alone and not on the denizens of the caves—unless you consider Pittsburgh an outdoor cave—and you would get several to agree with you. However, and notwithstanding, I shall ramble on, in my unpredictable fashion, cherishing the thought that perhaps I am furnishing a slight "Comedy relief" to the many strange, unbelievable, unthinking, profound, dismal and half-witted letters you must receive, I am sure, though, that you must receive some highly interesting and useful ones and will await with interest and a couple dollars for your book containing a collection of same, with, I hope, your always ready comments. That is one of the things I am forced to admire about you, your ability to always come up with an answer, no matter what the question. What puzzles me is your ability to weed out the crackpotted and smart aleck letters from those which are sincere—and no crack about what sort of a letter this is—I don't know my own strength.

At a risk of seeming to shovel out praise in a profligate manner, something I am very unapt to do, I must disagree with one of your statements in your letter which says quote, "I am not a good writer—". Now, to me a good writer is not one who uses precise English, flowery words, page after page of description of something like the left eyebrow of a swan, etc., etc., such as Galsworthy, Emil Ludwig, Thomas Mann and so on—most of whom bore me highly (I am no doubt revealing my lowbrow taste for the REAL literature) but a good writer is A. one who tells a story well, B. One who has a story worth telling, C. One who does not attempt to write over his readers low brows, D. One who has something to say and adopts the fiction form as the least painful way of getting his message across E. One who does not bore his readers with unnecessary wordage at so much a word—but that should give you an idea, for I could go on for several dozen more letters. There are some very good writers in the S.F. and Weird field and I honestly think their works compare favorably with many of the high priced name writers such as K. Roberts, B. A. Williams, U. Sinclair, J. Jennings all of whose works I like. Anyhow, finally we get to the point, I think you are as good as any of them—perhaps your style is not so profound or flowery but neither is it boreing, but you tell a story well and get your message, which is the real purpose of most of your stories, across—if you didn't, you wouldn't be getting so damn many letters—such as these. (Quote from R.S. —"Why did I ever take up writing.") Anyhow, R. I enjoy your works from the plain fiction standpoint, as well as from the "I wonder if maybe this guy ain't got something" standpoint. I may go into that later. (R.S.—"Not if I can help it.")

I have recently completed reading the "SECRET DOCTRINE" by Mme. Blavatsky which a friend lent me, and I might say that it gave me a hell of a tussle, especially when I got lost in some of those Stanzas. However, here and there I came upon sundry thought provoking items, many of which tie in with your theories. I shall not enumerate them, as you have perhaps struggled through this thing but I was interested in the mention of the caves and the various documents and other valuable items buried in same—also the fact that her theory of the Elder Giant Gods goes hand in hand with your argument. Of course, you could be, and probably have been, accused of borrowing some of her ideas and presenting them in fiction form, though I personally think not. (That's mighty decent of me). It's too bad this is so tough to read as there is considerable of interest in it, particularly to those who believe the bible is the last word in history, anthropology and some other big words.

I told you I was going to ramble on didn't I? Thanks for your word about the story "The Mound" I strongly suspect it might be in a book titled "The Outsider and Others" or "Beyond the Wall of Sleep" and not, as you hinted in "Sleep No More" which is an anthology edited by A. Derleth, who is not a bad writer himself, and also a busy little bee. I have this, by the way, in case you don't and would care to read same, though you probably have and did. (R.S.—"whatinell is he talking about"—A good question) I am not acquainted with Mr. McKenna—I recall a story you wrote in collaboration with him some time ago (and Mr. Fort, too) and was considering calling him up and asking some pertinent and impertinent questions, mostly about you, but decided that he wouldn't care to be bothered and so desisted—and don't you wish I had continued to desist. However, I don't think I would care to borrow the book from him as I wouldn't expect him to relish lending same, for I saw in a recent trade magazine that the "Outsider" is selling for $35.00 which leads me to wish I had purchased ten copies.

And speaking of Magazines, I received today, an obscure fanzine entitled "Other Worlds" in which you are mentioned in rather an unusual connection. In case you don't see this, I shall further bore you with a slight dissertation on the article which was entitled, "Fantasy In Music." On second thought, why should I work my fingers to the bone, I shall tear the page out and send it to you. I'm getting smarter every day—and high time. You don't need to return it. Well, I guess this will teach you a lesson not to pass out, to me anyhow, invitations to write but I think I have done you enough evil for the moment. I regret I have said nothing profound this time, but maybe I will do better in the future. (R.S.—"What future?") Anyhow, thanks again for your reply and if you have any spare time I will, welcome another note—even if of protest. Best wishes—Jack Cuthbert, Box 1736, Pittsburgh 30, Pa.

P.S.—As for Rabelais and the caves, I started him five times but never got to Chapters 25-35—Poor translation maybe—alibi. I may try again.—J.C.

*Dear Jack:*

*I'm only printing your letter so some of the other members will write to you so I won't have to do it. And you don't have to read the whole book of Rabelais to find Chap. 25-35 it's at the back end of the book—you turn the pages over till you find the numbers—see?—Dick.*

*P.S.—I can't read Blavatsky, either. And I didn't!*

Mr. Shaver:
Enclosed please find a postal note for the amount of one dollar in payment for the next two issues of the club magazine. I would again like to express my satisfiaction with the job you are doing. I was very sorry that both Mr. Chester Geier and Amazing Stories deserted you.

I read something in our local newspapers on March 22 which you may or may not have heard of. It was a short paragraph announcing the discovery of a substance called "rootin" which was described as an antidote for radioactivity. The word was given out by Mr. Von T. Ellsworth, Legislative Director of the California Polytechnic Institute. You came pretty close to it with "dunder" in the "Gods of Venus." The newspaper was the Newark Evening News of Newark, New Jersey.—Sincerely, W. Campbell Cameron, 145 Johnston Avenue, Kearney, New Jersey.

*Dear Mr. Cameron:*

*Neither Chet Geier nor Amazing has exactly "deserted" me. Chet has a series of westerns to get out, and Amazing is stocked up for six months.*

*About the substance "rootin" announced by Mr. Von T. Ellsworth, Legislative Director of the California Polytech—would some of you members get us the complete dope on this?*

*If radioactivity is age, and "rootin" is an antidote, and Mr. Ellsworth doesn't know radioactivity is age—maybe we could get some experimental work done on "rootin" by some of our scientific contacts who think age and radioactivity are blood brothers. I for one would like to see this lead hounded to its ultimate revelation—or disappointment.—your friend, Shaver*

Mr. Shaver:

In your reply to my information about the new substance, "rootin", you suggested that I try to gather more information regarding it. Well, Shaver, I tried. I went back to the newspaper "Morgue" and took another look through their files. Nothing. I went to the libraries of the cities of Newark and New York. Again nothing. Nothing under radioactive medicine, nothing under "rootin", no report under California Polytech. I sent off a letter to that school, asking for information, but it is a little too early to expect an answer.

Doesn't it strike you as just a little odd, that such an obviously important development as this should have received no more notice than a short squib on the last page of a newssheet? Maybe it turned out to be a dud. But read the article I enclose. It is the same I read two months ago. Have any of the other members mentioned it?—W. Campbell Cameron, 145 Johnston Avenue, Kearney, New Jersey.

Excerpt Newark Evening News
Monday, March 22, 1948
Newark, New Jersey

## BELIEVED ANTIDOTE FOR RADIOACTIVITY

VENTURA, Cal. (U.P.)—Rootin, a new substance believed to be an antidote for radioactivity, was disclosed unofficially today.

The new product reportedly was developed by scientists at California Polytechnic Institute. Legislative Director Von T. Ellsworth told a convention of the California Farm Bureau Federation that an official announcement was expected this week.

*READERS: Does it strike you, too, as odd that this substance ROOTIN, an antidote for radioactive poisoning (which may mean it is an antidote for effects of age) is receiving no more notice than if it were a cure for Athletes Foot?—Editor.*

Dear Mr. Shaver:

I hated to see Chet Grier (don't think that is the way he spells it) leave, but from the looks of this issue the loss certainly was not in the make-up of the magazine. Keep up the good work.

How's chances for getting a list of your other fans in this locality? Personal contact with them might prove interesting.

Here's another buck for the next two issues.—J. A. Francis, 1309 S. 38th St., Kansas City, Kans.

*Dear J.A.:*

*This is first issue entirely made up by myself, and Chet is a very big loss. We expect to get him back sometime in the future. I am putting your address on your letter to more completely satisfy your request for contact with Kansas readers. Hope the rest of the members will note that unless they do not wish their address published I will do so—and state whether or not they, wish their address appended to their published letters. It is desirable for it makes for a more complete exchange of info between members, but it could also mean you could acquire a "Horla" or two. It could also mean you would receive protection and help in time of need.—Shaver.*

## A VERY CLARIFYING LETTER WRITTEN BY A MEMBER

Dear Dick:

Have given your letter considerable thought these last few days. Especially your query in answering my second question. (What would you do?)

When you put it like THAT I can see YOUR point. Have considered what I would do if I were you under similar circumstances and end up realizing a person couldn't do much except as you are doing. By continuing to bring the facts before the public as you are—ultimately something is bound to come of it.

Just what it will be we shall have to wait and see. Perhaps closer contact with the friendlier elements to get the know how for combatting the others on more equal footing, or possibly the development of instruments and weapons of our own for that purpose.

Have also been considering your novel "Mandark" and its tie-in with Biblical accounts as well as forgotten accounts—books—of the Bible and the lost books of Eden.

You know, Dick, if a person will read all three carefully the probability of your accounts being authentic becomes more evident all the time. I would like to point out the way for belief to those more firmly entrenched in present day "religious beliefs than myself. According to a Jewish boy in my outfit overseas, the Jews have never accepted the Jesus Christ as the true Christ. Well, that agrees perfectly with your account. He wasn't the true Christ but only a human brought up and trained by the true Christ to act in his stead. Now the Catholics hold that when man dies he first enters purgatory to suffer for what sins he committed here could very well be the sufferings of those victims which you describe being tormented by the demented deros. Some of the protestant religions hold that there is no Hell for sinners (Seventh day adventists) and some hold to the old Hell's fire and brimstone preachings. Your version should be accepted and acceptable to all for those and other reasons.

I believe the trouble, Dick, that all religions have become so lackadaisy like that, most people don't believe in them anymore. (No! Ed.) They just accept them. They have pictured God as so far above mankind in perfection that He becomes too distant and vague for reality. And though the preachers thunder about the Devil and his imps of Hell people don't really believe in them anymore. (Well!) (Ed.)

If they did believe they'd have to start taking account of themselves and worry. Why worry?, they say. Have a good time, as long as you go to church on Sundays and outwardly pretend to believe in the whole business—why worry? Then go home and forget it because God is too perfect to be real and the devil never shows himself openly anyway. So there you have it. . . .

Now your account however, brings us Gods who are human although immortal and vastly more intelligent than mankind. And Devils who are horribly real and dangerous because of being demented and hating us here above.

In other words, your Elder Gods and your deros are something a person can believe in. The more one reads the bible and forgotten Books of the Bible the more one realizes that fact. Our religious interpretations of the Bible give us all a God who is perfect. Therefore whatever he made would be perfect. Then why did Lucifer rebel?

Because as you have told us the Elder Gods were not perfect only as comparable with mankinds present status. They were nearly immortal but they were still humans. And the effects of the sun brought the change that affected them and caused the suffering and misery since. Your account is something a person can believe wholeheartedly in.

Now that's off my chest I'll try and get down to earth again. Personally I haven't the money for undertaking expeditions in search of underground entrances either. My thought in asking just what you would do if you had money to go ahead with was should there be enough people to chip in if we had some specific undertaking in mind. Several persons have written to you they would be willing—(a hundred or so) and others would volunteer.

As you say, though, the impossibility of meeting this on equal terms is bad at present. We haven't the necessary equipment to detect or combat such ray mechanisms. An expedition underground without help and guidance from friendly tero elements could only end in disaster. Something will turn sooner or later however. Your continued expose must eventually necessitate their coming out in the open. When that happens I want to be on hand.

For my part I still have had no actual experiences to relate. Nothing that you could definitely put your finger on and say was the work of deros. There have been instances, however, in which things have happened that had to pass as natural occurrences. During the war especially. There are things which can't be shrugged away or explained as natural easily. Your accounts explained them though to my satisfaction anyway.

Now just one more question. Dick, you say you are in constant contact with these underground elements—are they friendly to us? Are you able to listen in on deros as well? Do you have intimate contact with a group who feel friendly toward us or is it that you can tune in on different minds? Hostile as well as friendly?

I can understand why even those that feel most friendly toward us would be reluctant to allow close intermingling and exchange of goods for ray mech, etc. Centuries of secrecy would account for that.

Undoubtedly you have tried and are trying to overcome that attitude. Having observed us here above for ages, they are probably timid about giving up such wonderful mechanisms and lose the advantages they hold over us. Perhaps if more of us could—(talk to them)— we could dispel their reluctance to come out in the open. Difficulties seem to pile up endlessly.

As I mentioned before you have a hard row to hoe in presenting your version of man's origin. Ordinary people dislike accepting the reality of Gods or Devils although the Bible upholds both. They say they believe in God or the Devil and let it go at that. It's too much effort to get down and really search of their truth between the lines. I am with you all the way, though, and I know there are many more who do agree with me. It is truly a tough nut to crack.—Sincerely, Laurence R. Davis.

*Dear Laurence:*

*Answering your one question—can I listen to hostile as well as friendly ray?*

*It's like this: There is a bunch would like to kill me, and I have to listen to them try.*

*There are those who won't let them, and I have to listen to them stop it. Also there are those who don't care, and make fun of both sides. I have to hear them. After a few years of an argument like that, personal friends of real closeness develop—but they seem to get transferred, or I move somewhere else, and it starts all over with different ray. I hate to take trips or move—one is more apt to get hurt then. The best proof that we have strong friends down there is—one never does get hurt, too badly.*

*Above all that there are those who work to keep any conversation with surface from betraying any info of value to us. That's tamper.. They scramble things by cutting in with foolish palaver, and telling lies.*

*But that isn't a good picture, because after first days, it's all silent—just a tension and watchfulness at certain times when certain rods are about. Certain times when I relax there's info comes through—about the ancient times, their way of life, whatever someone is thinking about or studying. I really believe this is a way station on a large interplanetary circuit with quite a bit of travel—or was at different times in recent decades. There is always a tension about them, a deadly feud—about—policies?—to stay alive with rods about and because—who knows what they are really up against they can't talk about. Maybe they're under an inhuman space race—how do we know. Sometimes I think that is true, even if they are human in appearance. Ruthless feudal lords—and kindly guilds and merchants—seems the picture. But the top is always out of sight. You see, Laurence—we're property.—Dick.*

Dear Mr. Shaver:

If it is caves you are interested in, how come you have overlooked this region of the country?

Over here, around Mt. Shasta and vicinity we have all types of caves and cave tunnels, all of them unexplored so far as I have been able to find out.

Woven around some of these caves are very interesting tales, circulating among the old timers.

Here they are, for what they might be worth to you.

They all boil down to this:

That the caves of the "Elk Flat" region lead to an underground village where strange people of a gigantic stature live, move and have their being.

That these people wear long brown robes, sandals, and bind their heads with a strip of cloth of the same color.

That they speak a strange language. That they have been seen at various intervals going to and from the "Elk Flat" caves at dusk.

I have been hearing these tales ever since I was a little girl. Please understand that these are just tales and I do not say anything about their truth.

I only think they are interesting enough to hand them down to you, in case you care to investigate their truth. The "Elk Flat" is there and the caves also.

There is still another interesting cave I would like to tell you about.

This one is located south west of Weed. It is shaped like a rail-road tunnel, and it is about 60 to 70 feet in height and 35 to 65 feet in width.

Upon inquiries made at the Mt. Shasta forest service, I was told that it has been followed for nearly a mile—without ever finding its termination. (Note, someone really went in a whole mile! They must have been tired. Shaver).

A few hundred feet west of this one there is still another one.

There is also the windy cave at Yellow Butte. This is surrounded by vegetation and is next to a side country road. There is also always a cold wind blowing up from it, wherefore its name.

There are also caves near the town of McCloud called the McCloud caves.

With these I am not very familiar, but I am sure someone at the forest service in McCloud can tell you how to get there.

There are still others but not very interesting except that there is ice in them most of the months of the year.

Take your choice if you are interested.

I am enclosing a map of the vicinity where the more important ones are. In case you print this letter please withhold my name.—Anon.

*Note by Shaver—The map enclosed is "Sacramento District, Shasta National Forest— California Region—U.S. Dept. of Agriculture Forest Service and I think you could get one by calling there at the forest service if you wanted it.*

Dear Mr. Shaver:

Since I first heard of the Shaver Mystery some months ago I have been boning up on it in your magazine and in whatever backnumbers of *Amazing* I could find, and have been extraordinarily fascinated by the whole business. Frankly, I still think it quite possible that you are as nutty as a fruitcake; but equally frankly, I am unable to find a single valid reason for arbitrarily rejecting any of your basic theories. Some of the details, no doubt, are shaky, but the only argument against the fundamental conception is that it does violence to established notions—and that has been true of every new idea from Copernicus to the present day. So, for what little they may be worth, I am contributing a couple of footnotes and an objection.

I am surprised that no one has mentioned William Blake in connection with the Shaver Mystery. He was, as you know, considered insane by his contemporaries because he claimed to see visions and to converse with "spirits," and the larger part of his writings is based on his visions and voices. Anyone with the patience to wade through his co-called prophetic books might, possibly, find references to the caverns. I lack that patience myself, for apart from a Miltonic grandeur of style they are turgid, chaotic, and practically unintelligible. In skipping through them, however, I happened to find a prose fragment, titled "A Memorable Fancy," that may interest you:

"I was in a Printing house in Hell, and saw the method in which knowledge is transmitted from generation to generation. In the first chamber was a Dragon-Man, clearing away the rubbish from a cave's mouth; within, a number of Dragons were hollowing the cave. In the second chamber was a Viper folding round the rock and the cave, and others adorning it with gold, silver, and precious stones. In the third chamber was an Eagle with wings and feathers of air: he caused the inside of the cave to be infinite; around were numbers of Eagle-like men who built palaces in the immense cliffs. In the fourth chamber were lions of flaming fire, raging around and melting the metals into living fluids. In the fifth chamber were Unnam'd forms, which cast the metals into the expanse. There they were receiv'd by Men who occupied the sixth chamber, and took the form of books and were arranged in libraries."

What does it mean? Your guess is as good as mine, or better.

Some of Blake's drawings, too, showing amazingly "lifelike" winged men, "angels", and what have you, may suggest a Shaverian interpretation. And in Leonardo's notebooks you will find detailed studies of the musculature of winged men, and of human legs with animals' feet, etc. Did Leonardo imagine these things, or was he, perhaps, drawing from life? And doubtless the same question could be asked of the evil monstrosities painted by Hieronymus Bosch.

And now for a brickbat, directed at the Shaver Alphabet. I wouldn't deny that all languages *may* have a common origin, or that the words in a language can be traced back to a fairly small number of primitive roots. But in applying your alphabet I'm afraid you will have to be a little more cautious and a little more gentle with the professors. In one of the discussions in *Amazing*, reference was made to Hogben's "Loom of Language"—now this is an excellent book, but it is deliberately a popular approach to the subject, and of course it often presents conclusions without giving the detailed reasons leading up to them. So although it may seem easy to stand Hogben on his head, the results don't hold water when you get down to specific cases.

The accepted views of philology rest on a chain of evidence that would be very hard to break up entirely. For example, you wouldn't deny that the English you and I write is descended from that of Carlyle and Dickens (despite the differences); nor that Victorian English is descended from that of Elizabethan times; nor that Shakespeare's language stems from Chaucers; nor Chaucer's from the Anglo-Saxon with the addition of French elements brought in by the Norman Conquest. From Anglo-Saxon back, it is true that there is no surviving written evidence for certain stages; but the reasoning that ties it in with Gothic, Greek, Sanskrit, etc., is exactly the same kind of reasoning that connects modern English with Chaucer's.

Try the same thing with French. It seems arbitrary, on the face of it, to say that French is descended from Latin. But it is not a question of professors' assumptions. It is a question of collecting a series of older and older French documents. Go back to Moliere, then to Villon, to the Song of Roland, to Chretien de Troyes, and finally to the Strasbourg Oaths, the oldest French manuscript, AD 842: "Si Lodhuvigs sagrament, que son fradre Karlo Jurat, conservat. . . . " It's Latin, but it leads to modern French a thousand years later, without a missing link.

There is additional evidence, apart from historical sequence of MSS, to show that the development of languages is a one-way street and that the accepted order cannot be simply reversed. Briefly, it rests on the principle that men do not arbitrarily adopt particles and endings which are in themselves meaningless. (Except, of course, in made-up languages like Esperanto.) That is, it is ridiculous to suppose that the letter "-d", which has no meaning by itself in English, was chosen from pure whimsy to be used as a sign of the past tense. If the "-d" that changes "love to "loved" is meaningless in English, then the only possible explanation of its use is that there was an older language, an ancestor of English, wherein the "-d" or its ancestor did have a recognizable independent meaning. And that is the case with Anglo-Saxon. The final "d" comes from a final "-dide", meaning "did"; therefore "loved", etymologically, is "did love"—and no other sort of explanation makes any sense; nor is there any question left as to which is the older language.

Apply the same reasoning to the case-endings that every student of Latin has to cram into his head: these endings, meaningless by themselves in Latin, can be traced back to the *older* related language Sanskrit, where they *do* have recognizable meanings as pronouns and prepositions.

If you want to assert that other languages come from something like modern English, then you will be obliged to claim that a meaningless final "-d" in English, by some sort of virgin-birth blossomed into a complete conjugation of "to do" in Gothic and Anglo-Saxon.

That's more than I can swallow. But if you want to take a list of Indo-European roots (there are only some 500) and apply your alphabet to *them*, then I might be able to go along with you.

These criticisms are meant constructively, and I hope you'll accept them as such.—Very truly yours, Stuart R. Sheedy.

*Dear Mr. Sheedy:*

*I think you have the time element confused in your language growth concept. If you remember I am speaking of pre-diluvean times, then you see I really have no argument whatever with modern ethnic exchange and mingling—nor with modern etymology at all. I only insist that if they concept of a time much farther back, and then boil down English to basic small sounding—sound-meanings—such as "mu" "On" etc.—what will result from the meaning still clinging to these, considered in the light of my alphabet—is something they must not miss.*

*Most of them make the mistake you make, that I am arguing with modern and medieval word collectors and labelers—I am not.*

*I am talking of the original spring of language as being something far, far different than a hairless ape in a cave—and hence must be so considered as a language sprung from degeneration of a once universal tongue belonging to a superior race.*

*You see there is in truth no argument between Shaver and modern etymology—we are talking about two different things. I am merely appending a most important preface—in time to their closer work—*

*I would like to take this up in detail, it is perfect proof of the mystery, but I always hesitate because it would bore so many and use all the space.—Shaver.*

*P.S.—If we could talk orally, could thrash this out. In applying the alphabet—remember it is a new tool, not a contradiction.*

Dear Friend:

I wish to write and tell you of a rather peculiar sequence of events that have been happening to me. I feel sure you will be interested for they portend in some ways to your own.

Well, while I was over to our State Library browsing around for some very old and out of print books, I ran across a set of books that had been printed in England 120 years ago and some of the pages had never been cut open, showing they had not been read. In these books I found a description of the caves of 'Ellora' which fascinated me for some reason, and I made a copy of this article. Some time prior to library experience I had sent to California for some book and received them four days after my copy of the cave had been made.

I suppose you are wondering about all this fitting into your experiences, well one of these books I received was the account of a man who called himself the Chevalier de B—— and this book was written 92 years ago. He told of starting to explore the caves of Ellora and of being caught from behind by giant hands who forced him to walk downward a long ways into the earth, and when he refused to go further, he was picked up with ease and carried as a child altho he claimed to be 6' tall. His experiences were as yours below the earth except for machines and monstrosities. Have you ever heard of the caves of Ellora and have you ever read Ghostland! If you would like my description of the caves I would be glad to send them to you.—As ever, yours sincerely, Rev. Irene Farrier, Charlotte, Mich.

*Dear Rev. Farrier:*

*I think I answered this letter saying Yes, but can't recall now. Am printing letter as I think others are interested in the old accounts of the caves of so many different kinds—and may want to correspond with you. Members remember we want to publish these antique accounts if you run on any not too lengthy. Or lengthy—we can cut them down. Such old books are out of copyright—could be used—and make interesting and convincing reading.—Shaver.*

Dear Mr. Shaver:

I find the club mag. very good, and hope that it will be as good in the future. Naturally no one could read of such things without developing some pet theories about them. I'm no exception. Since the recent advent of the flying disks, my pet theory has been developing about them. I don't know whether or not this will get past your waste basket or not, but. First there are some questions that have to be asked, not that you or anyone else could answer them. Mainly they run something like this. Why don't people, at least some people, with means, have any interest in the flying disks, flying "saucers" or flying whatever-you-want-to-call-them? Is the human race getting to the point where only money has any meaning? Are people so unimaginative that they can't conceive that there might be other races of beings in existance? And that those races might be so far advanced in sciences of all kinds, as to make our dabblings look like the play of some small child. For instance if you were to ask some great scientist to draw a picture of a space ship, he would probably draw a thing like a modern rocket. And why not? you ask, because most people have been brought up to believe that streamlining is the very limit, the ultimate of any type of vehicle. I sometimes wonder if any of these same people stop to think? Do they ever think of the fact that out in space streamlining is of no purpose whatever. Take some of the pictures that can be found in almost any pulp mag. The space ships are composed mostly of fins and landing skids. Good pictures, Yes, but not for the man who wants to go to the stars.

Well to get back to the theory. I have done a lot of wondering why, if the disks were space ships, they had that particular shape. And I've got what I think, is a good answer. Let's take it that we already have a drive that is usable. So now the problem of building the star ship itself. Since out in space you don't need streamlining why build a ship like that? Why not build it in the form of a sphere? There are a lot of advantages to this. One of them is that the drives could be placed to aim in all directions. And another is that a sphere incloses the most for the surface area. The outside skin, which has to be the heaviest for protection, would be uniform in shape, and would reduce the overall weight per area inclosed as compared to the other type of hull. But we still have the problem of shoving all the extras around in the gravity field of any planet that was investigated. So why not build the ship in sections? For instance, build the main part in the form of a cube with the corners rounded, then all the storerooms and living quarters could be in this section. Next build the drives in round sections, flat on one side and rounded on the other so that when attached to the main part of the ship the whole would be a sphere. This would give six smaller units containing all (or most) of the main drives and a number of control drives along with fuel for immediate use and the controls for the drives. And one large unit with storerooms, workshops and the main living quarters. When attached to the large section the units could be linked to form an integrated unit with any one of the sections as the master control. And when detached each small unit would have one (or more) of the main drives to give it power and plenty of speed. If the units are rather thin the drives, if they take up much longitudinal space, would be lying flat under the skin of the unit. The openings of the drives would then take the form of slits or other shapes. Or the drives could open out on a flat part of the edge, giving the unit the appearance of a rounded shoe heel. Upon approaching a planet the ship as a whole would be put into an orbit, and the units could drop free and go about the task of exploration with the extra baggage left out in space. A number of such units flying in formation would look like the things which Kenneth Arnold says he saw. What about it Mr. Shaver?—Sincerely yours, David T. Wilcoxon, 602 W. King St., Martinsburg, W. Va.

*Dear Mr. Wilcoxon:*

*I think your description of the nature of the discs could very well be the correct one, from other reports I have read of discs having a mother ship into which they merged. Hence am putting your letter in SMM.—Shaver.*

Dear Mr. Shaver:

In answer to your letter of June 21st, by all means publish my letter if you wish, and I am sure I will enjoy being contacted by people (queer sticks or otherwise) interested in, and believing, the same things we do. I get awfully tired of the closed mouth policy I have found I have to maintain with most people, on these subjects, or be branded as a crackpot. I imagine no one understands this fact quite as well as yourself.

Thank you for putting me on your list to help at any time. My husband and daughter will help also, and we shall do our best.

For many years I have believed that a race of people live at the earths core, also that we will be visited by another race from space some day. I have just seemed to know these things. I don't know how or why. I have always known the suns rays were harmful. We never spend a day on the beach, altho we live so near them. I feel very sorry for the thousands of sun bathers we see on the beaches every day, brown as Indians. They will not believe if one tries to tell them of the harmful rays. I know. I have tried telling a couple of friends.

It is amazing how all of my beliefs coincide with the facts you are now bringing to light.

I have just finished reading your wonderful, and tragic article "The Terrible Clock." How right you are, and I, for one, am not optimistic about our future. I wish I could be.

I have Rheumatoid Arthritis Mr. Shaver. The darn stuff picked me up some place in the deep south, during my five year sojourn with my husband, while he served with our illustrious U.S. Army. My daughter and I are trying to get the ray people to help me. I have a wonderful doctor who has kept me up and going, and from being crippled, but I don't like the idea of "Salts of Gold" in my blood stream. It is a drastic treatment. I will let you know how we succeed with the ray people.

I am always so happy to receive your letters. May everything shape up right for you to continue your wonderful work, and may all humanity bless you, as they certainly should.— Your friend (I hope), Lillian E. Wolff, 11936 Avon Way, Culver City, California.

Continued from page 35

But how can it be said that way? It is only a legend, and there are no rays sterilizing America, no stupid brutes making of the future of our race tree a bug-destroyed skeleton of leafless branches. There are no Asgards with the Apples waiting for the quick brain of an Idun to make them potent once again. There is nothing but Ivory towers, and stories of success in commercial sweat shops, and arty photo illustrations, and sleek rumps in silk, and stupid people following each other, following many big words, but none of them so truthful as these—it is Cant, and the empty words of posturing little men, and it is outmoded and unreplaced. Yet it is your education, and one must work with it to tell you new and terrible truths that you must know.

It was my education, too, once, but actual impact of events replaced the lies with the tremendous truth—we are a race of people defrauded of our true heritage of wisdom, bilked of our honest rights even in that our brains are mutilated by unseen rays! Our books have been so mutilated, too—just as have our brains.

We are a race of people invisibly enslaved and mocked and cruelly tormented and mutilated beyond words, physically, mentally and sexually—by things not worthy of our spittle in their faces!

And we are ignorant of it. We are unbelieving of the faintest whisper of the awful truth! We are pleased with our lot—and that lot is one of invisible slavery to brutal incompetents.

You ask for proof?

It can be seen in every phase of your daily life, in every newspaper, in every unexplained accident and murder and rape and beating. It can be seen on every side if you look with analytical, open eyes!

Oh yes they are that blind. They have been taught sweetness and light till they can't see bitter and dark. And life is full of bitter and dark, and we could do plenty about it, if people could admit that it wasn't all as lovely as they have been taught to think. People have become pitifully uncritical.

I don't agree.

That's just it. You can't agree, you've listened to the opposite view till your sense of truth is atrophied, you can't see a horrible truth when it hits you on the head.

Well, we'll suppose you're right. What about it. People wear rose-colored glasses —so what!

So when something needs to be done, like new sewage systems, hospitals that ain't grafts, doctors they can afford and all the many things people need and never get— they accept a lot of pretty words instead of real hard work and deeds. They accept the ugly thinking it is wonderful. They wear green glasses and they are fed saw-dust in consequence.

You can't say that about sex.

I can say it about sex. Love is a lot of child-like grasping for things that look pretty and turn out ugly. Sex is a false business all the way through, and people see the pretty side and forget . . .